Broken Sky

Part One

Other books by Chris Wooding:
Crashing
Point Horror Unleashed: Catchman
Kerosene

Look out for:
Endgame

Broken Sky

Part One

Chris Wooding

Cover and illustrations by Steve Kyte

SCHOLASTIC

Scholastic Children's Books,
Commonwealth House, 1-19 New Oxford Street,
London WC1A 1NU, UK
a division of Scholastic Ltd
London ~ New York ~ Toronto ~ Sydney ~ Auckland
Mexico City ~ New Delhi ~ Hong Kong

First published in the UK by Scholastic Ltd, 1999
This edition published in the UK by Scholastic Ltd, 2000

Text copyright © Chris Wooding, 1999
Illustrations copyright © Steve Kyte, 1999

Lyrics taken from *Flies and Honey* are reproduced by kind permission of Schema.

ISBN 0 439 01487 5

Typeset by M Rules
Printed by The Bath Press, Bath

10 9 8 7 6 5 4 3 2 1

"The maze began
On the other side of the sky"

Schema, *Flies and Honey*

Check out the

Broken Sky

website

www.homestead.com/gar_jenna

Broken Sky

1

The Creature Beneath

A scramble of dirt, unseen and barely heard.

Ryushi froze, his body going rigid. Knuckles bleaching, he gripped the hilt of his sword, holding it steady in front of him. Slowly, his eyes narrowed and he turned his head, looking over his shoulder towards the source of the sound.

It didn't come again. That would have been too much to hope for. He was lucky to have heard his pursuer at all.

Moving on soundless feet, he changed direction, slipping off between the tall, smooth trunks of the trees. The sun cut through the canopy of flat oval leaves in intermittent bursts, dazzling him for a second and then disappearing. High overhead, fist-sized kuja fruit hung in groups of three within their leafy pods, triplets of juicy purple ripening in the summer sun.

Sweat ran from his hairline down his forehead and neck. He blinked it away, squinting as a salty bead stung his eyes, then ran his hand through his spiky blond quills to shake off the excess. He couldn't afford any distractions right now. His enemy was too dangerous for anything less than total concentration.

Circling around, sliding past the narrow, willowy waists of the kuja trees, he trod lightly through the forest. If he was careful, perhaps he could get behind them. After all, his pursuer would be expecting him to keep on heading in the same direction. They didn't know that he'd heard them.

Now they'd see who was the hunter and who was the hunted.

Coming up on the spot where he'd heard the noise, his sword held ready, he reached out and pushed back a spray of leaves and looked.

Nothing. Nothing was there, except a cococo, foraging for grubs in the dirt and grass around the roots of a tree. It stood up on its hind legs as he emerged, large silver eyes fixed on him amid the jet-black fur of its face, head cocked quizzically to one side. It chirruped at him, then streaked up the bole of the tree, spiralling around it to the upper branches, its long tail following after.

Not here? Ryushi thought. *Then where...?*

His breathing stilled to almost nothing. The sound of the air passing over his lips seemed too loud. In the gentle rustle of the forest, amid the cries of the birds and the chattering of the cococos that lived in the trunks of the kuja trees, he listened.

There was a rumbling coming from behind him, so low it was almost inaudible, but getting louder fast, *faster*. He looked around frantically, but the forest was as calm and sunny as it had ever been. So where? Where was it coming from?

He looked down at the ground at his feet, caught in a sinking moment of realization, and suddenly he knew what was happening.

The dirt and soil burst open beneath him in a shower of earth, but he was already jumping, somersaulting through the air and landing ten feet away, his sword held two-handed before him in a ready stance. A hush descended on the forest.

Poised, he waited among the falling clods of muck, eyes searching for his attacker's next move.

For a time there was silence, punctuated only by the occasional thuds of dirt as they landed all around him. Then a deep bass moan emerged from the crevice that had opened in the forest floor, and a pair of enormous brown hands reached out and clutched the sides, pulling through the creature beneath. It came into view, first its head, then its shoulders, rising out of the ground until it stood at its full height, towering over Ryushi. It shook itself off, chunks of mud and grass falling from its massive shoulders, and then bellowed a challenge.

Ryushi took a step back, muttering an amazed oath under his breath. It stood at least twelve feet tall, a thing of dirt and roots, with wide, trunk-like feet and huge, crude hands. A shaggy mane of grass spilled over its face and along its shoulders and back. Its eyes were little more than holes, but they followed him cruelly as he backed away; and its mouth was a pit of jagged stones.

A golem. The biggest one he'd ever seen.

NO ESCAPE NOW, RYUSHI, it growled.

Ryushi only had a moment to blink in surprise before a fist bigger than his head came swinging at him, faster than he had expected. He cried out, throwing himself aside and rolling as it crashed into the ground where he had been a second before, making the trees shake.

He had barely gained his feet before a second swing was coming his way with a force that could pulverize rocks. He flung himself down, feeling the golem's fist whistle by inches above his head, blowing his hair with the wind of its passing.

This isn't right, it's too fast! he thought, dodging another wild swing that slammed into a tree and blew it to matchwood. It was pounding him under a constant barrage, never letting him get his bearings, forcing him to duck and weave just to stay out of its grasp. And, sooner or later, he was going to make a mistake, and that would be the end.

Again, again; narrow misses swiping past him, making him back off, not giving him room to swing his sword. He was panting, sweat falling freely from his brow as he tried to get away, get enough breathing space to…

His thought was cut short by a tree root, catching the back of his heel and making him stumble backwards, off-balance.

Uh-oh.

He raised his defences a split second before the golem's fist slammed into him. It was enough to deflect most of the force, but not all of it. He was thrown off his feet, hurtling into the forest, smashing through kuja trees like they were bamboo poles, and slammed into the flat side of a small cliff, cracking the stone. It was only the bubble of energy around him that stopped him from being pulverized like the trees.

He pulled himself free from the cliff and dusted himself off. The golem was thundering towards him, knocking trees aside with its shoulders, roaring in anger.

"Okay," he said quietly. "Enough."

He sheathed his sword and started walking towards the oncoming behemoth, the air around him beginning to hum as the spirit-stones along his back drew power from the earth, charging themselves like batteries. His eyes were flinty, calm in the face of the hurricane that was bearing down on him. He bunched his fist, feeling it begin to tremble as he channelled the power into it. Slowly, he began to run along the aisle of broken trees that had been left in his wake, picking up his pace into a jog and then to a headlong charge.

The golem, twice his size at least, bellowed as it rushed to meet him, a shambling hulk of detritus. Ryushi drew back his fist, still running, a battle-cry escaping his lips, turning into a yell as they clashed, smashing into each other with a force that levelled the forest around them.

For a moment, nothing could be seen but the haze of sawdust, and gently drifting particles of dirt and leaves as they settled in the aftermath.

Then a chunk of earth hit the ground. And another. In seconds, it was raining mud and roots, slapping heavily to the forest floor or crashing into the branches of the trees. The cococos chattered in panic, whirling around the upper reaches of the leaf canopy; but the assault on their homes was soon over and the forest quieted itself again.

Ryushi stood in the midst of a circle of fallen trees, his blond quills in disarray. There was nothing left of the golem. After a few moments, he fell to his knees, and then slumped to the forest floor, exhausted.

For a long minute, he was conscious of nothing but an aching bone-tiredness. Every ounce of energy had been drained from his body. Feebly, he tried to raise himself off the ground; but his arms trembled and betrayed him, and he slumped back, his cheek in the dirt.

"Gotcha," came a voice from behind him, and he felt something press into the back of his neck.

He rolled over to see a girl of about sixteen winters – the same age as he was – standing over him. She was holding a long, smooth pole to his throat: a bo staff. After a moment, she sighed, put the weapon aside, and dropped to her knees, sitting on his chest. She had small, pretty features, and wide green eyes which looked out from beneath her dark red hair. Her lips twisted in a wry smile.

"Y'know, you've got to learn to control yourself, bro," she said. "You could have beaten my golem with half the power you used. You can't overextend yourself like that; you'll just end up burning yourself out."

He shoved her off and got up. "Don't get cocky, Kia. It won't happen again."

"It's happened *six times* in a row," she replied, laughing. "I'll take my chances."

Ryushi began to walk away, but he had only taken a step before his legs failed him. He stumbled and had to sit down again hurriedly.

"See?" Kia persisted, from where she was lounging on the forest floor. "Weak as a kitten."

"So how come you've got so much better all of a sudden, anyway?" he said angrily. "That golem was the biggest you've ever come up with. And you've never been able to make them talk before."

"That was my special touch. Did you like it?" she beamed.

"It put me off," he replied. "I wasn't expecting it."

"You weren't supposed to. That was the point."

Ryushi lapsed into sullen silence.

"Don't get like that," Kia teased, prodding his back with her bo staff. "You just need practice."

"*You just need practice*," he mimicked cruelly in a whiny voice, bobbing his head from side to side as he said it. "Just enjoy it while you can, sis.

Once I get this little problem ironed out, you'll see who's better."

"Ooh, you're so *competitive*," she said. "I love the way you boys get like that. Really, it just *does* something to me."

"Funny," Ryushi replied, poking at the ground with the tip of his sword.

Kia sighed and got to her feet, leaning on her staff. "Stop sulking, anyway. We've got to get back home; Father and Takami will be back from Tusami City any time now, and we should be there to meet them."

"So what? I don't care," Ryushi replied stubbornly.

"Come on, you're not still sore at them, are you?" Kia said.

Ryushi got up from the ground unsteadily and slipped his sword back into its leather scabbard. "You know how much I wanted to go with them," he said.

"I know," Kia replied sympathetically. "But our time will come. Remember, Takami's a good couple of winters older than us. Father will take us when *we* come of age. Be patient."

Ryushi rubbed the back of his neck, where the drying sweat was making his skin prickle. "I just can't face him being smug. He's going to come back dropping all sorts of self-important hints about what they got up to when they were away. You know what he's like. Just because he's come of age, he'll be strutting round thinking he's the King."

"Hey, bro, don't let it get to you," Kia replied, slinging a companionable arm around his shoulder. "He's just *older* than you; he's not *better* than you. He's just jealous 'cause you've got a twin as wonderful as me and he hasn't."

"Yeah, *sure*," he said, seeming to shake off his gloom and suddenly becoming bright again. "His life must just be a misery without the *I-know-best* girl on his case all day."

"I *do* know best," she said, shoving him playfully. "That's why I keep winning."

Ryushi shrugged. "I'm hungry, anyway. You think Aunt Susa's made some of that sevenberry cake that Father likes?"

"Probably. When has Aunt Susa *not* had at least three cakes on the go?"

Kia looked around the clearing, examining the devastation caused by the clash between her golem and Ryushi. Fallen trees lay all about. High up in the branches, she could hear the angry chirruping of the cococos.

"I think we'd better find a new place to practise," she said. "There isn't going to be much left of this forest if we keep on coming here."

Ryushi walked over to where one of the newly-felled kuja trees lay and plunged his hand into the foliage. A moment later, he withdrew a thick leaf pod the length of his arm. Popping it open, he pulled out one of the succulent purple kuja fruit within and tossed another to Kia.

"It's not *all* bad," he said.

2

Cracks and Flaws

The day was wearing down to a sultry evening when they reached the top of the cliff edge. Kia got there first, Ryushi trudging along afterwards. The red orb of the sun was dipping beneath the western mountains, sending long shadows knifing across the panorama spread beneath them; and there they stood for a while, as they always did, looking down into the shallow mountain valley where their home lay.

The stables dominated the valley floor; an enormous wheel-shaped construction of faded red metal. Next to that was the looming circular bulk of the hatchery, squat and low. Other buildings crowded the wide artificial clearing at the bottom of the valley: fodder silos, workers' quarters, the long dining hall, storage sheds. And there, set a little apart, was the family house, nestling under a roof of wyvern-scales.

Osaka Stud, a small yet profitable stable compound run by their father, and the only home they had ever known.

"Is he back yet?" Ryushi asked, scanning the narrow road that ran up the thickly forested side of the valley and away through the mountains.

Kia squinted against the sun, trying to make out some of the figures that were busily milling between the buildings. "I don't think so." She brightened. "We might still be in time. Let's get down there."

Ryushi conceded with a tired sigh.

They set off down the dirt path that ran along the cliff edge, eventually curving off into the valley and plunging into the trees. The air was stiflingly humid there, but they pressed on doggedly until the forest suddenly gave way, and they emerged next to the hatchery, towering up to their left. They could hear the massive, dull rumble of the furnaces from inside.

A stable-hand, a boy of their own age called Mitamo, emerged from the small metal side door of the building. He waved a greeting to them, his skin glistening with sweat from the hot interior.

"Hey, Mitamo!" Kia called. "Has Father arrived yet?"

"Not yet," came the cheery reply. "He's sent a message saying he'll be a little late."

"'Okay, thanks." She turned to Ryushi. "Come on. We'd better clean up before he gets here."

They hurried up to the house, their feet scuffing up puffs of dust from the scorched earth. On their way, they waved to the other workers that they came across; but they met nobody that they knew well enough to delay them, and they were soon inside and out of the sun.

Their house was cool and shady, sheltered from the stark daylight by its overhanging wyvern-scale roof. There was nobody in at this time of the day; the family were out attending to their duties around the stables. Kia claimed the right to the first bath as the spoils of her earlier victory, so Ryushi was forced to wait. He dragged himself up the stairs, his hand trailing up the carven banister, and went into the bedroom that he shared with his twin sister and older brother.

For a long while, he sat on the edge of his bed, resting, looking around the wooden walls of their room. He felt drained. Kia had been right, much as he hated to admit it; he couldn't keep his power under control like she could. Getting up suddenly, he tugged his shirt over his head and threw it on the bed, then went to stand with his back to the long mirror that hung on the wall. He looked over his shoulder at his reflection.

Framed within the wrought-metal setting of the mirror was a boy of sixteen winters, his body lean and tanned, an elfin face looking out from beneath a bunch of thick blond quills. Running down his back, following the ridge of his spine, were six smooth elliptical stones, each one a clear sky-blue. Spirit-stones.

He reached around his back, and ran his knuckles over the cool surface of one of them, as if to check it for cracks and flaws. They seemed a little dull now, robbed of their usual inner light, their power expended.

He tutted to himself. Cracks and flaws? Spirit-stones were as near to indestructible as anything could be. No, there was nothing wrong with the stones. It was him that was flawed. He couldn't control them properly. At least, not yet.

"Don't worry about it," came Kia's voice from the doorway. She was freshly washed and dressed, her dark red hair still wet, tied in a ponytail with the fringe teased out. Ryushi started, embarrassed at being caught looking at himself.

Kia came into the room, sitting down on the edge of her bed. "It's natural, bro. Most people only have one spirit-stone to handle. Hardly anyone has more than four. You and I got six; so did Takami. It takes a while to get the hang of them."

Ryushi didn't reply for a moment, unconvinced.

Kia crossed her legs and looked at him. "Don't you remember Takami having the same problem at our age?"

Ryushi frowned. "Did he?"

"Sure he did. Well, he had different *stones*, but the principle was the same. He used to get so mad because he couldn't make them work the way he wanted to. Remember that time when he chased us both out into the forest, just because we interrupted his practising one day? You know, when we walked in on him trying to heat a cup of water and he couldn't do it?"

"That was why he chased us? How do you know?"

Kia smiled slyly. "Aunt Susa told me when I was helping her in the kitchen. I find out all sorts of things that way. After we left, he ended up torching the clearing. He could let his power *go* alright, he just had no fine control. Like you."

"He was really that bad?"

Kia's eyes flashed mischievously. "One time, he was trying so hard he made himself ill; he had to stay in bed for a week. At least you've never done *that*."

Ryushi grinned. There was silence for a moment, during which he studied himself again in the mirror.

"The bath's still hot," she said. "You'd better get ready. Father could be here any minute."

"Yeah, okay," he said, walking out of the room. When he got to the door, he stopped. "Thanks, sis."

"Anything to make Takami look bad," she

replied, but they both knew she was being flippant. Feeling better about himself, Ryushi went to take his bath.

He had scarcely managed to get himself dressed when Kia rapped on the door.

"Hurry up! He's here!"

His hair still damp, he opened the door to the bathroom and followed his sister as she ran down the stairs and out into the hot evening.

They got to the gates of the stable grounds just as the cricktrack emerged from the trees, coming down the winding mountain road. It was a squat, boxy vehicle, probably no more than twelve feet long and eight in width, that rumbled along on enormous caterpillar tracks. The tracks clicked loudly every time the seam passed over the guide wheel, giving the vehicle its name.

In the open-topped cockpit, they could see their father's young Pilot, Ty, his face set in concentration as he drove. In the Dominions – the kingdom in which they lived, which stretched south from the mountains to encompass an entire continent – the Pilots were not only the drivers of

19

the vehicles; they were also the power plants. Having no portable source of fuel, it was only those who bore the special green and black spirit-stones that could master the machines and give them life. Only they were permitted to enter the Pilot's Guild and become trained to drive vehicles such as the cricktrack.

Ty was serving an apprenticeship under the Master Pilot, Uji, who lived some way off in the mountains. Kia was quite fond of Ty, but he worked so hard that they rarely had a chance to see each other. Now she waved at him, smiling as he noticed her and waved back. Ryushi looked from her to him and back again with a wry expression.

Before the cricktrack reached the gates, their father's head popped out of the window in the flank. A moment later, the door slid back, and he leaped out of the slowly-moving vehicle and ran up to Ryushi and Kia, embracing them both in turn.

"My children! How have you been?"

"We've been fine, Father," Kia replied, beaming. "But what about you? How was Tusami City?"

"Oh, you know, business and business." He

took a step back, regarding them both with a broad smile on his face. His name was Banto; he was a bear of a man, with a grizzled brown beard and huge shoulders, but his eyes were gentle, and were creased at the edges with merriment. "Every time I go away, you two seem to double in size in my absence."

"Father!" Kia cried in mock-horror. "Don't say that! I'm at a tender and sensitive age."

Banto laughed, deep and booming. "You know what I mean, Kia. Allow a foolish old man the occasional slip of the tongue."

Behind him, the cricktrack had rumbled to a halt, and Takami stepped out with his slow, measured stride. Tall and slender, he had their father's dark hair – falling long and fine around his shoulders – and their mother's smooth features. Dressed in sombre black and purple, the heels of his boots crunched the stones underfoot as he walked to stand by Banto.

"Welcome back, Takami," Ryushi said frostily.

Takami gave him a nasty smile. "Good to *be* back, little brother," he said, knowing how much that title would irritate Ryushi.

21

"Shall we go up to the house?" Kia suggested, sensing the tension. "The rest of the family would—"

"Oh, I almost forgot," Banto interrupted. "I have a surprise for you both. Takami, would you fetch our little bundle?"

Takami bowed in his stiff, formal manner, and went back to the idling cricktrack. Kia and Ryushi craned to see what they had been brought, but their faces were a picture of surprise when Takami reached inside to help down a young girl of no more than eight winters.

"This is Elani," their father said to the twins, while the girl was still out of earshot. "She'll be staying with us for a while. I want you to look after her. She's a very special girl." Then he bent down to Elani, as Takami brought her over, and placed one massive arm around her shoulders. "Elani, this is Ryushi and Kia. They're going to look after you while you're here."

"Hi, Elani," Kia said, squatting down to Elani's level. Wide blue eyes gazed back at her, fascinated. Then, slowly, Elani pulled a lock of her long, straight hair out of her mouth, where she had been chewing it nervously, and reached for a lock of Kia's. Holding them together, strung up in the gap between their faces, she contrasted the dark red of Kia's hair with her own glossy black for a moment; then she dropped them, and her lips spread into an infectious smile.

"Hello, Kia," she said, in a small voice.

Banto beamed expansively. "Come on then, children. It's time for Aunt Susa's famous seven-berry cake."

Ryushi looked up hopefully. "She's made some, then?"

His father grinned. "She'd better have, or you'll be looking for a new aunt," he said.

Kia hesitated for a moment, glancing at the cricktrack. "I'll be along in a minute, Father," she said. "I want to ride with Ty."

"I'm sure I'll be quite busy enough with your aunt and cousins," Banto said indulgently. "But don't be too late, or you'll miss the meal."

"I'll just be a moment," she said, ignoring Ryushi's knowing look; and with that, she walked over to the cricktrack and left them to make their way back to the house.

"Hi!" Kia said brightly, as she drew level with where Ty was sitting at the front of the cricktrack, in the open-topped cockpit.

"Uhh ... hi," he responded, reddening.

"Mind if I ride with you?"

"I'm only going to the vehicle bay..." he said.

"I know. Do you mind?"

"No. I mean, I don't mind. Okay, sure."

She hopped up on to the hard metal bench next to him. "Nearly a full-fledged Pilot, right? I've never seen you driving before. Show me how you do it."

"Uhh ... okay, sure," he replied. He showed her the two levers in front of him, jutting from the cluttered instrument panel, a mess of brass dials and sliders. "Each one of these controls one of the tracks. Push forward to make it go forward, pull back to make it go back. You steer by making one track go forward faster than the other. It's easy."

"Easy? Then why do you spend so much time training?"

Ty gave her a sidelong glance. "Cricktracks are just the tip of the iceberg. You wouldn't believe the sort of things they've got *out there*." He gestured vaguely behind him, to the world beyond the confining peaks of the mountains.

"Really? And how do you make it ... y'know, *go*?"

"Oh, sort of like this," he said, and the cricktrack bellowed into life all around them. Kia tried to suppress a smile.

"Wow," she said. "That's pretty good. But how did you *do* it?"

He shrugged. "I dunno. I just did." He jerked a thumb over his shoulder, indicating his back. "It's all in the spirit-stones." With that, he took the levers and started the cricktrack forward, lumbering into the stable grounds.

Kia sat back and looked at him as he drove, basking the evening sun. She liked Ty. He wasn't at all like the other boys here, brash and full of themselves, as noisy as the wyverns they tended. No, Ty was different. With his untamed black hair and slender shoulders, he always seemed strangely faraway, quiet and thoughtful, reluctant to talk about himself yet full of hidden talents. In their secluded valley in the mountains, he was a fascinating contrast to the kind of boy she had known all her life.

There was another reason she liked him, too. She suspected he had a crush on her. Just her being near him made him blush and stumble over his words; and no matter how much she told herself she was only trying to be friendly to him, she couldn't help but enjoy the attention.

"How was the journey?" she asked.

"Umm ... it was okay. I made it there and back without anything going wrong. I guess that's a good thing."

"Of course it's a good thing," Kia said. "I imagine you'll be getting your full Guild membership soon."

Ty smiled nervously at her. "Maybe."

"You'll be leaving the valley then, I suppose?"

"Maybe," he repeated.

Kia sighed. "I'm happy for you, Ty."

"You don't *sound* happy," he said, glancing at her.

"I'm happy that you're doing well," she replied. "It doesn't mean I'm happy that you're leaving. But you've got so much to look forward to; you'll be going off, doing great things. You've already seen more of the Dominions than I have, and we're only the same age."

"Ah, it's not that great," he said. "Really. You're not missing much."

"You're just saying that to make me feel better."

"Yeah, actually I am," he said, suddenly animated. "It's *brilliant*, Kia. You can't imagine how much there is to see!"

Kia narrowed her eyes at him in mock-annoyance. "That was mean."

"Sorry."

"It's just that ... I mean, I'm not going to see you again. I hardly see you *now*, you spend so much time training or driving."

"It's not my fault," Ty said. "Besides, you're never around, either."

Kia looked apologetic. "You know what Father's like. He keeps us training all the time, keeping our skills sharp, learning how to fight, how to use our spirit-stones. I don't get a lot of time to myself."

"But why? I mean, at least I know why I'm doing my apprenticeship. What about you? Why do you spend all your time learning to fight?"

Kia looked out across the bustling stable, the people milling between the huge red buildings. Over the rumble of the engine, she could hear the screech of the wyverns. Feeding time for them, she guessed, looking at the fading sunset.

"He wants us to be ready for the outside world when we come of age. Like Takami. You know he won't let us leave this place until after our eighteenth winter? He says the outside world is a dangerous place, but I don't know about that. What do you think?"

Ty seemed caught, reluctant to contradict Banto, his employer. "Well, I mean, it's *strange*, sure. Strange and new. But I don't know if it's *dangerous*..." he said.

"Anyway, that's why he keeps us at our training. That's why we've all got six spirit-stones. Even with as much money as Father makes with these stables, it must have crippled him financially to buy that many for each of us. He says he wants us to be prepared..." She trailed off, aware that she was repeating herself.

They were coming up to the vehicle bay now, squatting alone in the midst of a dusty clearing, with trees rearing beyond it. The gaping doors in its façade were sliding open at their approach, revealing a low, wide hangar.

"I'd better go," she said. "I have to get to the meal. But listen, why don't we meet up tonight?"

Ty's face lit up for a moment, then crumpled in disappointment. "I can't. I have to go to Master Uji tonight; he'll be expecting a report. I won't be back for a few days."

"How many?"

"Three."

"Then I'll meet you three days from now, up on the clifftop at midday. How's that?"

"Okay, sure," he replied.

"If you're not there..." she said, narrowing her eyes again. "Well, just remember what an angry girl with half-a-dozen spirit-stones can do. I'll see you."

She slid down from the cricktrack and ran across the dusty ground towards the house. And though she never turned to look, she could feel Ty's gaze following her every step of the way.

3

On Mother's Grave

The air was filled with the hissing of steam, and the heat of the furnaces rose up in searing waves from the grilles in the floor of the hatchery. Ryushi stood on the balcony that ran around the edge of the circular building and watched the egg tenders below, protected by their thick wyvern-hide suits. Arranged around the floor, suspended in metal cradles, were several dozen huge eggs. Each was as long as a man, with a rough, leathery exterior and a yellow-white colour that reminded Ryushi of sour milk.

He looked down at them longingly. One day, when *he* came of age, one of those eggs would be his...

"Not for a while yet, little brother," came a voice from behind him, intercepting his thoughts.

When there was no response, Takami leaned on the railing next to him. "I was talking to you."

"I heard you."

Takami looked at him sharply for a moment; then his eyes returned to the scene below. "Really, little brother, this pathetic jealousy doesn't do either of us any good. I can't help being older than you. Is it my fault if Father won't let us go with him into the City until we come of age? Or that he won't let us have a wyvern of our own until then?"

Ryushi didn't reply.

His brother tutted. "Don't pine. He lets you and Kia fly some of the females, doesn't he? Be grateful for that."

"It's not the same, is it?" Ryushi replied. "Not the same as being Bonded. Not the same as having your *own* wyvern, watching it hatch, being with it as it grows, one that only you can ride..." He trailed off wistfully, then glanced at his brother and added scornfully: "But *you're* getting Bonded, of course."

"Next twinmoon," he replied. "You really can be immature, you know."

"Guess I'm not old enough to know better," Ryushi shot back.

Takami tutted again, but he didn't leave. For a long minute, they just watched the tenders ambling about between the eggs, rotating the cradles, cleaning the floor grilles.

"Why won't you tell me what you and Father did in Tusami City?" Ryushi said suddenly. "I asked you yesterday, but you wouldn't say." But his brother *had* dropped enough hints to make Ryushi burningly curious, however. Just as he had predicted.

"My hands are tied, little broth—"

"And stop calling me that!" he snapped.

Takami smirked to himself, satisfied that his needling had at last provoked a reaction. "Father made me promise not to say. And a promise *is* a promise." He paused, before adding: "Let's just say that it was something so important that only *men* can be trusted with it."

Ryushi bit his lip to hold back his retort. Unwilling to rise to the bait, he turned from the balcony and walked away in disgust. His teeth gritted behind his lips as he heard Takami's soft laughter follow him.

He came out of the hatchery into the cool night, stopping under the star-laden sky for a moment to take a few calming breaths. Glowstones bathed the stable-yard in their pale orange luminescence, kept in iron brackets that were studded around the sides of the buildings. A cool mountain breeze gently buffeted his face.

He'd known it would happen. Takami had only been back two days, and already Ryushi couldn't stand him. And with Kia disappearing off with that girl – Elani – all the time, he had little else to do but stew. Even Father had been busy, catching up on all that he missed out on when he was in Tusami City. "On business." What did *that* mean?

He'd always wondered about his father's business trips, but his questions had always been deflected and they had remained shrouded in secrecy. He'd been able to bear it while he knew that everyone else felt the same; but now that Takami knew the truth and *wouldn't tell him*, his curiosity had grown insufferable. And his brother was making it worse on purpose, taking his usual delight from annoying him. Maybe Kia was right;

maybe he *was* jealous of the close bond Ryushi shared with his twin sister. But even if he was, the knowledge didn't make him any easier to bear.

Frustrated, he crossed the dusty ground to the stables, where he knew his father would be at this time. He meant to get some answers, somehow. He was sure that he'd crack up if he didn't.

The stables were shaped like a wheel, with a hub, eight spokes and an outer rim. They towered above him, twice the height of the hatchery, their walls a dull red, patterned with patches of rust. He let himself in through one of the small worker doors.

It was dark inside. The glowstones that hung from the ceiling could only dimly illuminate the enormous aisles between the stables. All around him the soughing of the sleeping wyverns filled the air, the rhythmic sound of their breathing, the rise and fall of their enormous flanks. The musky scent of the females was thick in his nostrils.

It's breeding season, he thought as he walked into the aisle, a tiny figure beneath the looming metal stable-gates. Usually the wyverns roosted up in the mountains, coming back only for feeding; but during midsummer, the females were confined to the stables in the outer rim, and were let in one by one to the central hub, where the bull wyvern lived. The family only kept one bull wyvern at any one time, selling the others when they were young. Bull wyverns were liable to fight if they didn't get their own way; they had notorious tempers.

He walked for a while, his eyes straying over the massive metal gates that kept the wyverns in. They were opened, closed, locked and unlocked by devices of levers and pressure and steam that he did not understand. Like so many other mechanisms that formed an essential part their daily lives, they were a product of the Machinists' Guild in the West. The Machinists were notoriously secretive and reclusive, and their services did not come cheap; but their handiwork was evident everywhere in Osaka Stud, from vehicles like the cricktrack to the dispensing devices in their fodder silos.

After a time, Ryushi heard the sound of talking up ahead, drifting through the orange-stained darkness to his ears. Picking up his pace, he went onward. As he neared, he recognized the voices of Banto, Kia and Elani; eventually, they came into sight. Elani was sitting on Kia's shoulders, peering through the grille in one of the stable-gates.

"But what do you *do* with them?" Elani was asking, her voice full of wonder.

Banto laughed. "Wyverns are very profitable creatures, Elani," he boomed, his voice echoing along the aisle. "Their scales can be used for all kinds of things; the shells of their eggs make fine light armour; their talons – which we have to clip once a year – can be used to make expensive ornaments. And there is always a demand for young bulls, whether for racing or for riding; King Macaan himself has some of mine in his private flight."

"Macaan..." Elani repeated, something distasteful in her voice.

"*King* Macaan," Kia corrected, laughing. "Don't say it like that. He's a great leader; he keeps the Dominions a safe place for people like us to grow up in."

"But he's—"

"Elani..." Banto interrupted gently. "No buts.

King Macaan has done a lot of good things for the land since he came to power. For instance, you know we used to have different thanes for different provinces? Collectively they were called the Dominions, and that's how this land got its name. Well, it was an inefficient way to run things, with thanes sometimes falling out and fighting. So when Macaan became King, he unified the provinces under one rule. Things are better now."

"Yes, Uncle Banto," she replied reluctantly, with an expression on her face that indicated she'd heard it before and didn't believe it then, either.

Ryushi winced. Now she was calling him *Uncle*? Who was this girl, anyway?

He recalled what Kia had told him: that she was an orphan who had been adopted by Hochi, one of their father's friends in Tusami City. Hochi had asked Banto to look after her for a few months, while he attended to some business. But in the few days since she had arrived, Elani seemed to have adopted *them*, calling Banto her uncle and Kia and Ryushi her cousins. She seemed to have attached herself especially to Kia; and Kia, who had never had a younger sibling, was enjoying every minute of it. They spent almost every waking moment with each other. Ryushi couldn't help feeling a little left out.

"Look, Elani; it's Ryushi," Kia said as she saw him approaching.

"Hi, Cousin Ryushi," she said, smiling sweetly. Ryushi thawed immediately, forgetting his previous grumpiness.

"Hi, El," he said.

"Cousin Kia was telling me about how you blew up a golem *this big*," she said, spreading her arms so wide that she nearly lost her balance and fell off Kia's shoulders.

Ryushi looked at his sister and raised an eyebrow. Kia made a tiny shrug, her expression saying: *Okay, so maybe I exaggerated a little.*

Banto laughed his foghorn laugh, his eyes falling on Ryushi. "That big? Really? You must be getting better."

"Slowly," Ryushi replied modestly, embarrassed at being the centre of such admiration.

"Slowly is the best way to learn, son," Banto said philosophically. "It means you've time to learn everything else along the way."

Ryushi looked down at the ground, suffering a moment of uncomfortable silence before he said: "Father, I need to speak with you." The tone of his voice told Banto it was something serious.

"Why don't we go and have a look at the big bull wyvern?" Kia said to Elani, tactfully excusing herself.

"Yeah!" Elani replied enthusiastically. "Is it bigger than the girl wyverns?"

"Oh, it's *huge*," Kia said to her, as she carried Elani away. "It's so big, it could just stomp on you and it wouldn't even notice."

Elani's giggle diminished as they walked into the dim light, leaving Ryushi and his father alone in the aisle, with only the vast sighs of the sleeping wyverns for company.

"I've noticed how Takami has been with you, son," Banto said, his deep bass voice a comforting rumble. "I think I can guess what this is about. Our trip to Tusami City. Am I right?"

"It *is* that, Father," Ryushi said, forcing himself

to look levelly into Banto's eyes. "But it's more. I don't know if it's because I notice little things more as I grow, or if… It doesn't matter, anyway. Father, there's something you're not telling us. And it's not just that you don't want us to get involved in your business until we're old enough to understand it, like you always say. It's all these trips away, all this secrecy … all these letters you write, all these people who turn up at the stables and then disappear, and you always tell us that they're just old friends but they're *not*. Forgive me, Father, but even I can see that by the way you are with each other."

Banto was silent, his expression unreadable behind his thick beard, his eyes regarding his son. Ryushi wasn't sure whether it was anger, pride, sadness … or all three. He wanted to stop now, but he couldn't. He had to get it out of him. He needed to know. In a quieter voice, he continued.

"I've always accepted the things you've told us, Father, even if I didn't quite believe them. But how could you swear Takami to secrecy? How could you let him in on it all, and carry on treating me and Kia like children, telling us stories about what you're doing as if we didn't know they weren't true? Even Elani, Father. Are you really looking after her for Hochi while he goes away? You have to tell me."

For a moment Banto didn't say anything … but then his broad face split into a smile, and his eyes filled with tears. He laid a huge hand on his son's shoulder.

"I'm sorry, Ryushi. If I'd have known how bright my children had grown in my long absences, I wouldn't have deceived you. But if you don't want to be treated like a child, then act like an adult now. Accept that the reasons I have for not telling you what I do are good ones, and trust your father. When the time comes, you will know; and perhaps you'll wish then that you hadn't been so eager to find out. There is a big and dangerous world out there, more dangerous than you know, and one day you will have to face that. I just want you to be as ready as you can be."

Ryushi looked hard at his father, his eyes pleading. "Then … you can't tell me *anything*?"

"No," said Banto. "I wish that I could, I truly do. But I can't. I won't deceive you again, but I cannot tell you until you are ready. Until you are ready to *understand*."

Ryushi's face hardened in anger. "And Takami? Was *he* ready?"

His father's eyes dropped. "I fear not," he replied, sorrow in his voice.

Ryushi snorted and turned away, stalking down the aisle.

"Son!" Banto called after him.

He stopped. "Yes, Father?"

"I know you're angry now. I know I have no right to ask, after what I have just said. But you must promise me something."

Ryushi's jaw tightened. He didn't reply.

"The girl. Elani. Guard her with your life. *Promise* me."

"I swear on Mother's grave," he said quietly. "If you wish me, Father. I will guard her with my life."

"Thank you, son," Banto said, and his voice, so quiet, seemed suddenly terribly fragile in the orange twilight.

4

Unfamiliar Markings

The moons stood out huge against the clear night sky. The vast, mottled white disc of Cetra shone high over the valley, carving its inexorable way towards the far-off dawn. Its smaller sister, Mauni, was half-hidden behind the teeth of the mountains, tinging the peaks of the trees with its pale, washed-out blue.

Silhouetted against the larger moon, Kia sat on the edge of the cliff that looked out over the stables, one leg hanging over the drop, the other drawn up to her chest. Next to her, two tiny golems – no more than three inches high and formed in the perfect likeness of humans – were wrestling with each other. After a time, she swept them away with her hand, watching as they tumbled over the cliff and dissolved into a loose shower of dirt; then she turned her face back to the moon, and was still, lost in thought. Tears stood in her eyes, shimmering there briefly and finally dropping from her lashes to her cheeks.

She had been there for some time when the sound of a footstep made her turn. Coming up the path was the small figure of Elani, wearing a loose white dress that made her look like a spectre in the moonlight. Kia blotted her eyes with the back of her hand as the young girl sat down next to her.

"Come back from the edge," Kia said quietly. "You'll fall."

"You've been crying," Elani observed, ignoring Kia's advice.

She sniffed, managing a wet half-smile. "There's no hiding anything from you, is there? What are you doing out at this time?"

"I sneaked out," she replied. "I didn't want to stay in that room."

"Mother's room? Why not?"

"I'd rather sleep in the workers' quarters."

Kia blinked. "Elani, why? You're our guest."

"I tried to tell Uncle Banto, but he wasn't

around," she said, picking up a stick and drawing shapes in the dirt at the cliff edge.

"He was inspecting the mountain roosts today," Kia said. "What did you try to tell him?"

Elani twisted the hem of her dress into her fist. For a moment, she looked undecided what to say; then she looked up at Kia and said: "I don't like mirrors, Kia. Please don't ever put me in a room with mirrors."

"What's wrong with mirrors?"

"I'm afraid of them," came the reply.

Kia was about to say something, but she sensed that Elani didn't want her to pry any further. Instead she settled on: "Okay, if that's what you want. But tomorrow night, we'll arrange a different room in the family house for you. A guest of ours isn't going to sleep in the workers' quarters."

They sat there together, watching the moons, before Elani took the lock of hair that she had been chewing out of her mouth and said: "Cousin Kia? It's your mother, isn't it? Why you were crying?"

A warm night breeze stirred the air around them. Kia blinked back fresh tears that threatened, and felt her throat tighten.

"How do you know about my mother?"

Elani shrugged. "I just know."

Kia spared a glance for the young girl by her side. This wasn't the first time that Elani's manner had seemed far older than her chronological age suggested. Then, as now, her eyes would seem to lose the naïve innocence that she carried around with her, and become strangely altered, becoming ... well, she didn't know. But there was something hidden within this girl of eight winters, something that Kia had never seen before in someone of her age.

"What happened?" Elani asked, her wide, dark eyes looking up at Kia.

Kia sighed, taking a deep, steadying breath before she began. As she talked, she gazed into the cool white glow of Cetra, and the moonlight limned the curve of her cheeks and chin and throat.

"It was a year ago this month," she said. "Mother and Father often went off together on his business trips. In fact, I think it was on one of his trips that he met her. But this particular one, we were waiting for them to come back; Aunt Susa had let us stay up late. It was a night like this one. And when we saw the cricktrack coming, we ran out there to meet it. But only Father came out." She paused, feeling the tears begin to prickle at her eyes again. "And all he said to us was: 'Your mother isn't coming back, children.' And that was all we ever knew."

"He never told you?"

"He told us later that she had died. Until then, we'd thought she'd just forgotten us, or that she didn't want to come back. We thought it was our fault. I guess that was why Father had to tell us that much. But he's never spoken of it since; and we have to respect his silence."

Elani's head bowed, the breeze stirring her sable hair. "Oh," she said.

"I took it much worse than Ryushi. He's accepted it by now. It's enough for him that she's gone. But for me ... I want to know *why*. I want to know what happened. Because I'm sure that I couldn't take it if the same thing happened to Father ... if he went away on one of his trips..."

"And didn't come back," Elani finished for her. There was silence between them for a moment.

Then, with a rustle of clothing, Elani edged closer to Kia and leaned against her shoulder.

After a time, Kia said: "How did you know I was up here?"

"I just knew," Elani replied.

"That's what I thought you'd say," Kia replied, and they stayed and watched the moons rise for a while before going back to the house.

The sun was high in the sky when Kia returned to the clifftop, and it beat down hot on her bare shoulders. The air was humming with the sound of insects, and the nearby kuja trees basked in the brightness. Her troubles of yesterday had seemed to dissolve in the peace of sleep, and this morning she felt exhilarated at the glorious day surrounding her. She had chosen a midriff-revealing top to wear today, which was a reasonably daring move, for it let the sun sparkle on the deep, earthy red of those spirit-stones further down her back. Dominion etiquette dictated that to ask another person about the properties of their spirit-stones was unthinkable; but while displaying them through choice was hardly taboo, it was still frowned upon by the old and proper. Right now, though, Kia didn't care. It was too nice a day.

She had spent the morning helping out around the stables, as she often did. Banto never insisted that the twins and their cousins joined in with the running of the stud, but Kia enjoyed being around the wyverns, and mixing with the workers. Today, she had been feeding the females with Mitamo. He was not exactly the type she'd pick for a friend, but here in the mountains she couldn't afford to be choosy. She met few enough people as it was.

Now she had returned to the clifftop that she and Elani had talked on the night before to wait for Ty to keep their appointment. She had got to their rendezvous a little early, because she wanted some time to soak up the blazing summer sun; so she lay down on the warm, dry grass, pillowed her head with her hands, and relaxed while she waited for him to arrive.

It wasn't long before she heard the sound of someone approaching, coming up the path from the valley. Shading her eyes from the sun, she looked to see who it was. She was slightly surprised to find that it was Mitamo.

"Hi, Kia," he said.

"Shouldn't you still be working?" she asked.

"You won't tell, will you?" he said, with a conspiratorial grin.

"I guess not," Kia said.

"I knew you wouldn't," he said, sitting down next to her. "What a day, huh?"

"Yeah," she replied, looking at him oddly.

"Just lying in the sun…" he observed.

"Waiting for Ty," she finished.

"Pilot Ty?" Mitamo asked, surprised. "He your boyfriend?"

"No, he's not my *boyfriend*," Kia replied, annoyed. "Why is it whenever a girl and a boy are friends, they have to be *together*?"

"Hey, don't get mad," Mitamo said, grinning nervously. "I didn't think he really was. I was just asking. I wouldn't have come up here if I thought he was."

"Meaning what?" Kia replied, her voice becoming flinty.

"Meaning … y'know…" he said, his hands

waving suggestively as if he was trying to get Kia to finish the sentence so he wouldn't have to. "I mean, this morning ... working together ... we really hit it off, right?"

"And...? " Kia said, beginning to suspect what he was about.

"And ... when you said ... when you said you were going up to the clifftop, I thought you meant..."

"Thought what?" Kia snapped, angry. "Thought I meant for you to follow? Thought I meant we could... Oh, you guys make me so *mad.*"

Mitamo scrambled away from her as if stung, and began to back off; but she swept her hand out, and suddenly the ground at his feet coiled up around his ankles and held him fast.

"H-hey, if this is about your *last* boyfriend ditching you, that has nothing to do with me!" Mitamo protested, flailing his arms. "Let me go!"

"It's not about Areki!" she replied, getting up and advancing on him. "Although he was just the same as all the rest of you. *Why* can't a girl be nice to a guy in this place without it being a marriage proposal?"

"Marriage!" Mitamo cried, as if burned. "Now, hold on! I never—"

"All I was doing was being friendly to you this morning!" Kia continued, steamrollering him. "At what point did that become *I want to bear your children, Mitamo?*"

"*Children!*" he fairly screamed, then began to babble rapidly in panic: "Listen, if I've misunderstood you then please accept a full and complete apology and I can only blame it on the declining lack of moral standards in our generation (at least that's what my uncle tells me) although that in no way excuses my deplorable behaviour and I thoroughly deserve any punishment you see fit to deliver…" he sucked in a huge breath "…but *please* don't make me *marry* you."

Kia stood there, amazed, for a few seconds. Then she turned away from him and said tiredly: "Just get out of my sight, Mitamo," and the restraints around his ankles crumbled to powder. He was gone by the time she turned back, scampering away like a rabbit.

Her mood now thoroughly soured, she sat

back down cross-legged on the grass and scowled at the sun-baked ground.

"Hey, was that Mitamo?" came a voice nearby, and she looked up and brushed away a frond of red hair to see Ty approaching her cautiously.

"Yeah," she replied.

"Are you alright?"

"Did he say anything?"

Ty scratched the back of his neck. "I dunno, he was running so fast. It sounded like 'Flee the devil woman,' but I can't be sure."

"That'd be right," Kia replied morosely, picking at some grass. She got up suddenly; he took an involuntary step back. Smiling at his wariness, she said: "I'm not going to hit you. I just wanted to walk. You want to walk?"

"Okay, sure," he replied.

They took the route away from the cliffs, heading up into the kuja trees which almost exclusively dominated this part of the mountains. It wasn't long before their ambling route took them up a long, well-used trail that wound through a wide cleft in the rock. The walls rose high and close on either side of them, and the ground underfoot was loose and gravelly.

"Where are we going?" Ty asked after a while, interrupting the smalltalk they had been making.

Kia stopped and looked about, then frowned. "I don't know; I wasn't really thinking. The roost is up here. Shall we go and look?"

Ty smiled. "Why not?" And they continued.

As they went, Kia told him about her encounter with Elani last night, and what had happened with Mitamo the following morning. She left nothing out; he had always been easy to talk to.

"It's just ... I mean, the other girls at the stable tolerate them, even if they don't like them. But I can't do that! Why should they be allowed to treat us like marks on a scorecard? Why should I have to watch what I say to a guy in case he tries to pounce on me? It's their whole *attitude* that—"

"Is this about Areki?" Ty interrupted.

"That's what Mitamo said!" she cried. "Why *should* it be?"

"Umm ... it just sort of follows, that's all. You were never like this before you two broke up..."

"Before he *ditched* me," Kia said, casting him a sharp glance. "Be honest."

"Okay, sure … umm … and since then you've been … I dunno, unwilling to play The Game."

"What Game?" Kia asked tersely.

"You know … the great philosopher Muachi. *The Game of Man and Woman.* Master Uji made me read it when I was younger."

"I suppose I missed that one," Kia said, the anger draining out of her a little. There was no point getting angry at Ty because of what Mitamo and Areki were like. He wasn't the same as them, and he was just being honest. Still, it stung to have the truth pointed out to her like that.

"Doesn't matter. You wouldn't have followed the rules anyway," Ty said brightly.

She smiled. "I hope not, if those guys are playing the same set."

And then suddenly the high rock walls on both sides fell away, and they were standing in the roost.

Ty's jaw dropped open. He had never been to the roost before, or at least not since he was very young. His training as a Pilot had taken up too much of his time. It had always sounded like an unremarkable place; but he had reckoned without the sheer immensity of what faced him.

The cleft that they had been following right-angled off into a thick ledge, along which a road had been cleared for cricktracks. Facing them across the vast gulf of a canyon was a huge rock wall that dropped away into the blackness at his feet and soared high above him. Gaping, irregular caves studded the surface, a hundred entrances into the enormous natural warren in the mountainside. And everywhere, the creatures themselves, soaring against the blue sky overhead, or spiralling up from the depths of the canyon to disappear into the caves.

"These are the pregnant females, and males that are too young to cause trouble with the bull," Kia said, smiling at his wonderment.

"They're incredible," he said, his head tilted up to the sky. "I'd forgotten what it was like ... just to see them flying like this."

"Here, watch this," she said, and with that, she drew out a small, diamond-shaped stone from where it hung on a thin chain around her neck. "They love these." She held it in front of her lips and whistled, varying pitch until she found the right frequency. The stone began to hum and vibrate.

"Is that ... a Bonding-stone?" Ty asked.

"Yeah," Kia replied, breaking off from her whistling. "Me and Ryushi got one each when we were five. It splits in two equal halves. When you get Bonded, one half goes on the wyvern's forehead, the other goes on your own. It's like you... Oh, wait, here comes one now."

Ty watched in wonder as a young male, who had been watching them intently ever since Kia had brought out the Bonding-stone, swooped down from the mouth of a cave. Its enormous wings carried its heavy body easily through the air; a second, smaller pair in front of them conspired with its long, split tail to steer it. With a gentleness that seemed to defy its size, it swept down and landed on the wide road next to them.

Ty was still. He had never been this close to an untethered wyvern. His eyes ranged nervously over its huge form as it regarded him with an intelligent gaze. Its skin was a leathery black; but its head, back, chest and the upper side of its wings were covered in rigid white plates of a bone-like armour. It stood on two legs, with inverted knees like those of a horse and massive, three-toed claws. A long, snakelike neck ended in a blunt, rounded muzzle of black, surrounded by a skull-like mask of white bone. Its eyes were a bright amber, and no pupils swam inside them.

"What's it called?" he breathed.

Kia laughed, a high, cascading sound. The wyvern's head curled round on its long neck to look at her. "I don't know. We don't name them unless they're Bonded."

"It's got to be... Hey, what's going on?"

Ty was midway through his sentence when suddenly there was a ripple of collective movement across the roost, a synchronized action like a flock of birds taking off together. As one, every wyvern in the roost had suddenly looked up, and had either stopped still or were lazily gliding to a perch.

Kia frowned, dropping her Bonding-stone pendant back inside her top. "I don't know. I suppose..."

She was cut off by the explosive blast of wind as the nearby wyvern suddenly launched off the ledge, swooping down into the depths of the canyon and disappearing into one of the caves. The rest of the wyverns were following suit, running or flying into the mountain warren, until after a few moments the frenzied sound of movement died into silence, and the roost was deserted.

"What was *that* all about?" Ty asked Kia, his eyes ranging nervously across the cave mouths.

"Something's frightened them," Kia said, concern in her voice as she looked up at the sky. "Without the stronger males around, they're skittish."

"Wait…" said Ty, following her gaze. "I think I can hear something…"

Over the soft hiss of the breeze, a *swooshing* noise was approaching, gradually getting louder.

"What *is* that?" Ty asked, the question addressed to nobody in particular.

He was answered by an ear-shattering screech, and three wyverns exploded over the mountain tops, screaming by overhead. He shuddered, his hands flying to his ears. They had unfamiliar markings on their underbellies, and they flew in strict formation. On their backs, he could see red-armoured riders, their faces blank visors, with long black braids that streamed out from their helmets.

"Those are war-wyverns," Kia said, confusion and concern in her voice. "They're from the King's fleet."

"The King's? But why?"

Kia's attempt at an answer was drowned out by the arrival of another trio of wyverns, following the last.

"What are they doing here?" Ty cried over the racket raised by their wings as they swooped past, his hair whipping around his face.

Kia looked at Ty, horror growing in her eyes.

"They're heading for the stud!"

HOCHI

ZU-JIN

I GERDI

5

Not Without

"El!" Ryushi yelled, rushing along the corridor of the house. The walls shook around him, planks bucked beneath his feet, and puffs of sawdust belched from the ceiling as it threatened to cave in from above. One hand against the wall to steady himself, the other holding his long, ornately wrought sword, he forged through the chaos. Outside, the screeching of the wyverns and the noise of the barrage assaulted his ears from all sides.

"Ryushi!" came the answering scream. "*Ryushi!*"

He threw himself at the door of their mother's old room, which had become Elani's temporary bedroom. The door came off its hinges as he shoulder-charged it, swinging inward at a skewed angle, and Ryushi burst through.

Elani was crouched behind a chest of drawers, trying to hide herself in the pitiful cover it provided. Looming over her was . . . what? Ryushi caught his breath. It seemed to be a man, tall and spindly, but wrapped head to toe in all kinds of rags, metal bands and belts. Even the face was mummified; no sign of the flesh beneath showed through. Its features – if that was what they could be called – were made of dull metal. One eye was a flat lens, the other one telescoped out to the distance of about an inch as it saw Ryushi, focusing with a whirring noise. A circular grille substituted for its mouth.

"Get *away* from her!" he cried, shoving his way across the room, the tumult outside forgotten for the moment.

A strange mechanical whine of feedback escaped the creature, and it turned away from Elani to meet this newcomer, moving in a disconcerting, insectile way.

"Ryushi, look out! They're dangerous!" Elani warned from her hiding place.

As if to prove the girl right, the stranger's fingers spread wide, and with a sudden *shrik*, sharp metal nails appeared, each about two inches long. It came on, weaving towards Ryushi. Ryushi circled, his sword point hovering in front of him, keeping the bed between them, leading the stranger away from Elani.

Then it sprang, leaping across the bed towards him, one razor-tipped hand swinging at his throat. He sidestepped, bringing the pommel of his sword down hard on the back of its head as it lunged by. It hit the ground in a roll and flipped back up on to its feet.

+++ **You are interfering with an emissary of King Macaan** +++ came the curiously buzzing voice of the stranger. +++ **Your treason will not go unpunished** +++

"You're lying," Ryushi said, his eyes never leaving the other. "What would King Macaan want with an eight-winter child?"

The stranger cocked its head to one side, its telescopic eye whirring. +++ **King Macaan's reasons are his own, and not privy to the son of a *traitor*** +++

As the last word was spoken, it ran for him, feinted at his head and then struck at his belly.

Ryushi drew back just in time, the finger-blades opening a line of four parallel slashes in his shirt. A second blow followed instantly, snapping out towards his face, but at the last moment turning into an elbow that cracked across his jaw, sending him spinning away. He fell on to the bed, managing to draw his legs up and flip backwards before the stranger's finger blades shredded the blanket where he had been a split-second before.

Elani screamed, but Ryushi couldn't spare her any time now. In one fluid motion, he landed on his feet on the far side of the bed and brought his sword down in a double-handed swing at the stranger's skull. The mummified thing caught it in its left hand.

For a moment, Ryushi was speechless, unable to believe what he had seen. His sword should have cut through the stranger's hand like putty. And in that short second of hesitation, the stranger's other hand came up, bunched in a fist, and struck the flat of the blade halfway down its length, smashing it in two.

Ryushi cried out as the blow jarred him up to

the shoulder. He let the useless hilt drop from his stunned fingers; and then his face set, and he prepared to face the enemy barehanded.

The stranger threw aside the sundered blade in his hands. +++ **Stop this idiocy. I only want the girl. You can stay to suffer the same fate as your father** +++

"I promised my father that I would protect this girl with my life," Ryushi said, his voice low and threatening. "That means, to get to her, you go through me."

The stranger paused, another short *wheep* of feedback escaping its mouth-grille. +++ **So be it** +++ came the reply, and it dropped into a ready stance.

"Ryushi, don't!" Elani squealed, tears of fright running down her face. "I'll go with it!"

"Shut up, El," Ryushi snapped tersely. "You're not going anywhere."

+++ **I beg to differ** +++ said the stranger, lunging across the bed at him. He stumbled back, taken off-balance by the speed of the attack, and crashed into his mother's old dressing-table. The large mirror that was part of the table had been covered over with a drape as a temporary measure to satisfy Elani's fear of mirrors until they could move her to another room; but now, as he banged into it, he noticed that the drape had come loose, and their reflections were revealed. Elani screamed again, picked up a make-up box that had fallen off the dresser, and threw it with all her strength at Ryushi's attacker. But her aim was wide, and she hit the mirror, smashing it. The stranger's head whipped around to look, and then turned back to face her, fixing her with a flat, glassy gaze of penetrating dread.

That distraction was all that Ryushi needed. He threw a punch right from his shoulder, sweeping it under the metal features of the creature and into its jaw, feeling the satisfying jolt in his arm as it connected. Thankfully, he hit flesh and not metal, and the creature was knocked off its feet with a mechanical howl.

It flew across the bed, landing with a crunch on the floor on the other side. Ryushi pounced after, his fist raised for the finishing blow, but the creature had regained its wits with alarming speed, and scrabbled aside so that he missed, crashing into the floor where it had just been. It rolled over on top of him, throwing him over and pinning him to the ground, its hands drawing back for a twin strike at his throat. They darted downwards, the razor tips promising the end; but Ryushi's hands shot up, grabbing the creature's wrists and arresting them in mid-lunge.

"Mis*take*," he said, and sent the full power of his spirit-stones through his palms.

The creature screamed, a high-pitched sawing noise, as the energy coursed into its body. It fought and thrashed, but Ryushi's hands were clasped hard, trembling with the power that swept through them. Bucking and shrieking, its wail ascended in pitch until it became almost unbearable . . . and then, in an explosion of white light that filled the room, it was silenced. Outside, the bombardment continued, a little further away now; but inside, there was no noise at all.

Elani ran from her hiding place, coming up to Ryushi, throwing her arms around his neck and crying: "You did it! You did it!"

Ryushi returned the hug, but he barely had the strength to hold the little girl in his arms. Once the

69

floodgates had opened, he hadn't been able to stop; he had drained himself totally. And how could he defend her, now that he was weak as a child himself. . .?

But there was one thing that dominated his mind, plaguing him insistently. Something the creature had said.

His father was a *traitor*?

"What are they doing? What are they *doing*?" Kia cried as they arrived at the clifftop, her hands on either side of her head as if to contain the pressure of disbelief within.

Osaka Stud lay in ruins in the valley beneath. Great gouts of smoke billowed from a huge hole in the hatchery roof. Almost a quarter of the outer rim of the stables had been reduced to a twisted mass of metal. The screeching of the trapped wyverns inside was audible even at this distance; but it was not enough to drown out the bombardment going on at the far end of the valley.

As Kia watched in horror, the red-armoured Riders swooped their wyverns down towards the fodder silos. Seated behind them in the harnesses were Artillerists, recognizable by their dark green lacquer, and the long, thin muzzles of their force-cannons mounted on saddle pommels. As the wyverns swept past, the Artillerists unleashed a volley of force-bolts, near-invisible except for the rippling wake they left in the air, which smashed into the silos with deadly force, blasting grain and rice in all directions.

Closer by, the wyverns were beginning to land, and from their backs were clambering the black-armoured foot-soldiers of the King's Guard, clutching long halberds. Workers fled in terror from them as they forged into the buildings and struck down those that they found inside.

Kia didn't wait for Ty to catch up with her. Instead, she turned, and sprinted headlong down the cliffside path that led to the stud. "Wait, Kia!" Ty shouted after her; but there was nothing that would stop her now, and he could only follow.

She ran down through the fringe of forest that surrounded the stud, and emerged next to the hatchery, tears of fury blurring her eyes. The air was thick with the dust that had been kicked up by the attack. The heat was no longer comforting, but seemed to clog an atmosphere that was already crowded with screams.

"Father!" she cried suddenly, and began to run towards the family house, a vague shape cloaked by the murk. Ty was forgotten behind her, following as best he could.

"That's one of them!" came a shout from ahead, and suddenly two Guardsmen were running towards her, appearing out of the haze. Their segmented black armour made them look like beetles; their faces were hidden behind smooth metal visors, with dark lenses for their eyes. Wielding their halberds – thin metal poles with curved blades mounted on the end – they headed towards Kia.

A shriek of frustration and anger escaped her lips, and she swept her hand out at them. The ground beneath their feet gaped open with a terrific rending noise, and something huge loomed over them before crashing down on their heads like a tidal wave. A moment later, the ground was back to normal; but the men were gone. Kia ran on, paying them no more attention, thinking only of her father and her family.

By skirting the edges of the forest, she was able to avoid being seen again after that. The distance between the hatchery and the family house was not far; she covered it in less than two minutes, though they seemed like hours to her. Arriving at the front door, she pushed in recklessly, heedless of any danger to herself.

"Father!" she shouted as she ran into the hall, which was covered now with rubble and debris. "Ryushi! Father! Are you here?"

"Up here!" came a small voice. Elani. Breathing a moan of relief, Kia ran up the stairs, taking them two at a time. Elani was standing amid the bent and broken chaos of the landing.

"Elani! Where's Father and Ryushi?"

"Ryushi's in there!" she said, motioning with her eyes as she wrung her hands in distress.

Kia hustled her back into their mother's bedroom, to find Ryushi propped up against the bed, breathing heavily. He looked up feebly at her as she came in. It took her only the length of a glance to realize what had happened.

"He saved me," Elani said, clinging to her thigh.

"And drained himself doing it," Kia added, hurrying over to her brother and helping him up, supporting him across the shoulders. "Is anyone else in the house?"

Elani shook her head.

"Come on, then. Let's get out and find Father."

The sound of running footsteps preceded Ty's sudden appearance in the doorway, out of breath.

"They're surrounding the stud!" he gasped. "They're not letting anyone get out!"

"We've got to find Father!" Kia repeated.

"We've got to *go*!" Ty cried.

"I'm not leaving without him and Takami," Kia said, steel in her voice.

Ty paused for a moment, indecision crossing his face. Then: "I saw them. They were heading for the stables."

"Then that's where we're going," she replied, and with her arm around her brother, she led them out of the room.

When they got outside, the bombardment had all but stopped. The sounds of shouting and running, the clash of metal and the screams of the trapped wyverns in the stables filled the air, coming at them out of the haze of dust. Kia had grabbed her bo staff on the way out, and Ty had his curved shortblade; to them would fall the task of protecting the weaker two.

"Keep together, and go fast," Kia said, her voice cold with determination. To Ty, she said: "If anyone or any*thing* gets in our way, don't hesitate. It's us or them."

"But they're the King's—" Ryushi protested wearily.

"I don't *care*," Kia snapped. "Now come on!"

Together, they stumbled through the choking cloud of dust, heading across the compound to the stables. Dark figures ran by them, silhouetted against the bright sun, black ghosts in the yellowish murk. Ryushi was beginning to get a little of his strength back, enough to help Kia out in her task of carrying him. Elani stayed close, frightened eyes glancing in every direction. Ty followed along behind, keeping a watch on the little girl.

"Stop right there!" a gruff cry sounded from

their left. Kia released Ryushi instantly, leaving him to stand unsteadily while she readied herself. The hulking form of an armoured soldier rapidly gained definition as he raced towards them.

"Make a golem, Cousin Kia," Elani urged.

"No time," she replied, hammering the end of her staff on the ground.

The ground at the feet of the running soldier suddenly dipped, becoming a sinkhole. The sudden drag on his feet as they plunged into the shifting earth tripped him, and the weight of his armour sent him crashing to the ground. Kia jabbed her staff hard between the plates of armour at the base of his skull. He twitched once and then lay still, unconscious. She raised her staff again, ready for another strike, her teeth gritted. . .

"Kia, don't," said Ryushi gently, laying a hand on her arm.

She glared at him, but he met her gaze calmly. She slowly lowered her staff.

"The stable doors are just there. Let's get inside," he said.

"Come on!" urged Elani.

Together, they crossed the remaining distance, surrounded by the clashing of steel and the cries of the wounded, and then plunged into the cool stables, shutting the metal door behind them.

6

The Prize Above

Inside the stables, the screeching of the wyverns was terrible. They were frightened at being trapped in their pens. They could sense the presence of the King's wyverns, and hear the sounds of fighting outside. They could smell the dead females that had been housed in the part of the stable that had been demolished. And it was making them angry.

Elani screamed in fright as the tall metal oblong of a stable door dented outward with an explosive punching noise. Ty took her hand, hurrying her past it.

"They're getting mad," Kia said. "They want out."

"What are they doing?" Elani cried, hearing another impact against the metal.

"You know all that tough, bony stuff around their heads, El?" Ryushi said. She nodded. "Gives them one mean headbutt," he finished.

They raced along the cavernous aisles, battered on all sides by the terrific howling of the wyverns and the deafening crashes as they threw themselves against their doors.

"They'll hurt themselves!" Elani cried. "We have to let them out!"

"They'll be okay," Kia said, her jaw set. "Did you see which way Father was going, Ty?"

"I assumed he'd be heading for the hub, where the bull is," Ty said.

"But we can't just leave them here!" Elani wailed, continuing her own train of thought. "They'll be killed!"

"Elani!" Kia snapped. "Just shut *up*!"

"No, wait," Ryushi interrupted, halting them all. For a moment, his eyes locked with his sister's, unable to understand her sudden harshness. Elani looked wounded. "She's got a point. We have to let them out."

Kia glared at him.

"Half of them are newly pregnant, Kia. And

letting the wyverns out will create enough confusion so we can all get out of here."

"I'm not going anywhere without—"

"I *know*," Ryushi hissed. "We've heard that one, sis. Now why don't you go find Father and Takami, while I open the stables?"

"Don't be stupid," Kia said tersely. "With the mood they're in, if you let the wyverns out, they'll stampede. Anything in the corridors will get crushed and whoever's in the lock-chamber will be trapped there. We can't *help* them."

"I'll go," said Ty.

They all looked at him.

"Didn't you hear what I just said?" Kia asked.

"Okay, sure, we can't let the wyverns out. But listen; Banto might be heading for the hub, right? Maybe he wants to save his prize bull, I don't know. But the only way to get the bull out of there is through the iris lock in the roof. Now, you can open it from inside the hub, but first you have to go to the lock-chamber to pressure up the mechanism. It's a system to prevent anyone accidentally letting the bull out."

"So, what, you think he might be going for the

lock-chamber?" Kia asked impatiently.

"Worth a try. You're too weak, Ryushi. You can only just run. I'll see if I can find him in the lock-chamber. You guys get to the hub; I'll meet you there. *Go!*" And with that, he sprinted off in the other direction.

"What is *with* you, sis?" Ryushi accused, turning back to Kia.

"I've already lost one parent," she said, iron determination in her voice. "I'm not going to lose another."

Ryushi dropped his eyes. Without a word, he set off in the direction of the hub. Elani and Kia caught him up in a few steps, and they were gone, disappearing into the vast aisles of the stables.

The outer rim, where the females were housed, was connected to the central hub by eight spokes. The spokes were long, metal tunnels, big enough to lead a wyvern down, with grilles overhead that threw their shadow-pattern across the squares of sunlight on the floor.

They were halfway along one of the spokes when they heard the clinking of running soldiers, and a patrol of six black-armoured Guardsmen appeared at the rim end, arriving in the direction they had come from.

"It's them," one of the soldiers said to another. "Get help."

Two of them hurried away; the other four chased after the fleeing trio.

"Halt there!" came the shout from behind; but Kia, Ryushi and Elani ignored it, continuing their run.

"Do something, Kia," Ryushi hissed.

"My stones aren't *inexhaustible*," she panted. "If we can make the hub gate before them, we can lock them out."

A bolt of concussion smashed into the wall next to Kia's shoulder, the shockwave warping the air around it. She swore and stumbled, turning to look over her shoulder. Another of the guards was levelling his halberd at them; and from the hollow metal tip, another bolt seared out, passing overhead.

Ryushi glanced desperately up at the hub gateway. It stood open at the moment, the archway beckoning them onward. The solid metal gate could be dropped like a portcullis from the outside, sealing all the doors around the hub, to prevent the bull wyvern from escaping if ever he got violent.

But it was too far away. They would have to fight.

"Kia, we don't have a choice," he said breathlessly. "Do it."

She stopped dead, turning around, and hammered the butt of her staff into the ground. Her spirit-stones glowed in the bare skin of her back; the dark, fiery red of magma. With a terrible grinding and cracking, a huge ripple spread from where she had hit the ground, hurtling up the corridor towards the Guardsmen. The walls of the tunnel buckled under the earth's convulsion, screeching in protest. The wave swept into the men, flinging them off their feet, and they smashed heavily to the ground.

Kia felt a weakness clutch her. She was nowhere near strong enough to keep using her spirit-stones like this. For a moment, she leaned on her staff, swaying; but she held herself together, and turned back to the others, who had nearly reached the gate. She herded Elani and

Ryushi through, and then slapped her palm against the pressure-release switch. Steam billowed from the archway with a deafening hiss, and the gate began to clatter down rapidly. Kia ducked underneath and through, and the heavy gate slammed shut behind her a moment before a concussion-bolt from one of the guards slammed into it with a *whoomph*.

They were standing on a wide balcony that ran around the outside edge of the circular room. Eight gates, including the one they had passed through, studded the outer wall at even intervals. On the other side of the room, between two of the gates, a wyvern-sized elevator door stood open, the cross-hatched metal bars raised out of sight. It was there to let the females – who were led along the spokes and around the balcony – down into the bull wyvern's domain.

Beneath them, there was the pit. Some of the glowstones had been smashed, and their illumination scattered or extinguished by the anger of the creature below. It had been roaring and thrashing as it caught the scent of its females dying, and heard their distress; but now it had fallen quiet, as it smelt the presence of newcomers. It was just possible to see the bull wyvern stalking around below, as an edge of its bone-armoured wing slid through the weak light of the glowstones. Waiting.

"What about Ty?" Elani said, seeing that all the gates around the hub had slammed shut at the same time as the one they had come through.

"Where's Father?" Kia cried, ignoring the younger girl, her jaw set as she cast around purposefully for a sign of him.

Another *whoomph* of concussion struck the door at their backs, making them jump reflexively; but the door held.

"They'll be coming through any second!" Ryushi said urgently, grabbing his sister's arm.

"The pressure-release switch is an emergency measure that shuts all the hub doors in case the bull goes berserk. They can't be re-pressured except at the lock-chamber – so they can't be opened from anywhere else," Kia said, her eyes roaming the interior of the hub. She paused to look blandly at Ryushi: "If you'd ever bothered to work the stables, you'd know that."

Ryushi let the comment pass without a response; they didn't have time for bickering now. Besides, he understood that Kia was fraying fast. She was a strong girl, but not where their father was concerned.

The assault on the door fell silent. Ryushi listened in anticipation of the next blast, but it never came. Even Kia halted, waiting.

"They'll be back," Elani said, her high, small voice breaking the silence. "They'll bring bigger force cannons to break through."

Ryushi looked at her in surprise, taken aback by how certain of her own opinion she sounded; but Kia barely gave the comment a moment of her attention.

"Ty said they'd be *here*!" she shouted, and there was an edge to her voice that Ryushi had never heard before.

"Calm down, sis," he said gently. "They might be—"

"They're *nothing*!" she cried. "They're not in the hub! And we've trapped ourselves in here without them!"

"But what about Ty? How's he gonna get in?"

Elani persisted, returning to her previous question.

"He'll see what we've done when he gets to the lock-chamber," Kia said dismissively. "The pressure-levers pop up when the gates shut. He'll open one of them and meet us. And he'd better have the others with him." She was standing against the balcony rail, her eyes scanning the semi-darkness below. "Father?" she shouted. "Are you down there?"

There was no reply, but the huge presence below stopped moving, and in the tiny orange glow she could see its long neck raised up towards them.

"We're not *trapped* in here," Ryushi said, walking across the balcony to stand next to his sister, and looking up to the dark roof.

Kia followed his gaze. After a moment, she realized the gist of what her brother was saying, and her eyes became chips of ice as she rounded on him angrily. "You're suggesting we get out of here? Without waiting for Father and Takami? What kind of son are you?"

Ryushi held her gaze steadily. "The kind of son who does what his father would want of him," he replied. "Do you think he'd want us to stay here, on the chance that he might arrive, when we could save ourselves?"

"*Save ourselves?*" Kia hissed. "Where is your loyalty?"

"I *am* being loyal," he replied, his face suffusing with anger at the insult. "Father made me promise to protect Elani with my life, and that's what I'm going to do. And that means getting her *away* from here."

Kia stared at him, her eyes blazing, her body tensed. For a long moment, they stayed like that.

"There's nothing we can do, Kia," Ryushi said. "We're stuck here, with only one way out. Any second now those Guardsmen are going to be back. We can't help anyone else. We have to trust Father and Takami to get away themselves."

Still Kia didn't move. Even the wyvern below them seemed to be frozen with the tension.

"Kia," Ryushi said, putting his hands on her shoulders. "Even though we're twins, you've always been like a big sister to me. You've always been the calm one when I got angry; you've always been the one who helped me when I got frustrated. But Father and Takami don't need you to look after them. Elani *does*. And I can't get the harness on that wyvern unless you help me."

"We're going to *fly* out?" Elani exclaimed, her voice a mixture of fear and excitement.

"They'll be okay," Ryushi continued, his soothing, reasonable tone slowly penetrating his sister's mind. "You have to believe that. We have to trust them to get themselves away to safety. Just as they have to trust *us*. I know how you feel about Father; I feel the same. But think how he would feel if we were caught, and he escaped."

And gradually, as he spoke, the hardness in Kia's expression faded, and she looked for a moment like a lost child, her head hanging in despair; but a moment later her eyes fired with determination, and her head came up again. She brushed her red hair back from her face and looked at her brother.

"Then what are we waiting for?" she said.

The sound of Ty's footsteps were a only faint tap in the vast, echoing dimness of the stables, but they were by no means the only sound to break the silence. All around him, he could hear hurrying feet and the clink of armour. Shouted, incoherent commands swept past him, phantom voices of unseen enemies. Outside, the airborne assault had stopped completely, and the cries of the dead and dying on the ground had dwindled into a few isolated pockets. From before and behind was the terrifying din of the wyverns, desperately trying to escape the stables which had become their prison. But here in the wreckage, the wyverns were silent.

He stumbled on, negotiating a lance of metal roof-strut that lay atop a pile of rubble. This part of the stables had taken a direct hit from a force-cannon, and the roof had caved in, destroying the pens on the outer edge of the rim. The doors on the other side had been blown inward by the force, and the concussion of the blast had seen to the rest of the wyverns.

Ty found tears coming to his eyes as he scrambled over the rubble, not only because the stench made him gag but because of the terrible loss of life here. His encounter with a young wyvern at the roost, only a short while earlier, had left him with a renewed sense of wonder at these magnificent creatures; and to see them so callously slaughtered wounded him deeply. But what was worse was the sound of the battle outside, as the stable workers tried to defend themselves with what pitiful weapons they had against the might of the King's Guardsmen.

He tried to shut out the smell of the dead creatures, tried to block the cries from outside. Why was this happening? *Why?* Osaka Stud was being destroyed, and its inhabitants slain or rounded up, and nobody had any idea *why*!

He clambered onwards, nearing the end of the rubble-slide that partially blocked the corridor, cutting his hands and feet in his haste. Scrambling down the far side of the obstruction, he saw the lock-chamber door. Like all the workers here, he'd done a mandatory season's general work before being allowed to specialize, so he had a small knowledge of the stables, and he recognized the dull, iron shape of the door instantly. It had narrowly escaped the obliteration, and stood unharmed a little way down the corridor, on the outside wall. The sound of screeching wyverns was louder here, too loud to hear any approaching footsteps. He trusted to luck, hoping that there would be nobody near by, and ran for it.

But fate was not with him this time. He was not halfway there before the corner curved away and he pelted into sight of a Guardsman, the black-lensed visor snapping around at the sound of his footsteps. Too late to stop now, Ty thought, as the Guardsman called out a challenge and raised his halberd to waist-height, pointing it at him. Moving on instinct, he dived as the concussion-bolt slammed past him, feeling it sear by an inch above his shoulder. He came to his feet and ran for the lock-chamber as the Guardsman aimed again. Forging through the deafening clamour of screeches, he pulled open the heavy door and slammed it to behind him, ramming the thick iron bar home to secure it as he heard another bolt shriek past.

The lock-chamber was a small room, lit by a single glowstone. Usually, it was closely guarded, to prevent anyone but the lock-keeper from touching the equipment; but there were no guards here now. Banks of levers, a tarnished bronze-grey, ran along one wall. They were thick and heavy, little more than rude shafts of metal, and at the base of each was inscribed the name of the door it operated. He hurried over to the panel and bent close, reading over the names. Each of the individual stables was marked on; but a master lever controlled all of the eight sections of the outer rim, enabling all the stables to be opened and closed at once. The whole thing was powered by a combination of steam power, counterweights, and intricate devices and mechanisms that only a member of the Machinists' Guild would understand.

Breathing heavily, one side of his body bathed in orange light, the other in shadow, he waited. Silence. What was the Guardsman doing? The door was too thick to hear footsteps through. Perhaps he—

Ty jumped as a concussion-bolt smashed into the door, filling the small room with a deafening ring. The bar dented inwards, but held steady. Just.

It was then that he noticed the row of nine levers, standing on their own. Beneath them, a metal plate said simply: HUB. They were in the up position, which was unusual. That meant the hub doors were closed.

He smiled faintly to himself, and the smile had no humour in it. Well, they had done as he had intended, and shut themselves in the hub. It would be the only safe place for them, with the Guardsmen running around everywhere. It was also the only place they could get out.

He wished he hadn't had to lie to Kia. He wished he had *really* known where her father was, or even Takami. But in truth, he hadn't seen them at all since the attack had begun. She wouldn't have listened to him if he hadn't deceived her. She wouldn't even have tried to get away. She would have gone looking for her father, and she would have been caught, and maybe killed.

He couldn't allow that to happen. Not to her. To see those depthless green eyes widen in terror, for that sleek, perfect neck to tighten into a scream. . . He wouldn't be able to bear it. Ever since he had met her, he had loved her from afar, never daring to get too close for fear of frightening her off, waiting, waiting for the right time. . .

Well, he'd waited too long. He had been too obsessed with becoming a Pilot, too obsessed with *making* something of himself, something that he felt would be good enough to offer to her, good enough to be worth having. . .

And now it was too late. Now he was trapped in here, with no way out. Still, he might have failed at that, but at least *she* could get away. At least she might escape this catastrophe unscathed.

Another bolt slammed into the door, buckling and twisting it inward. One more, maybe two, and the Guardsman would be through. Hurriedly, he found the lever that released the iris lock in the hub and pulled it, feeling it slowly give with a heavy clank.

"With the mood they're in, if you let the wyverns out, they'll stampede. Anything in the corridors will get crushed. . ."

Kia's words. Ty looked at the thick metal door, and thought of the black-armoured figure outside. He thought of all the other Guardsmen, who must be swarming through the stables. Maybe they were battering on the hub doors even now.

I wish I could have been there with you, he thought.

He turned to the bank of levers and took a deep, sighing breath, making his chest swell. Squeezing his eyes shut, he put his hand on the master lever, and as he did so he saw, in a moment of premonition, the chain of events that his action would set in motion: the rampaging wyverns storming the corridors; the Guardsmen trampled and stomped underfoot; and him, safe and yet entombed in the lock-chamber, for the heavy door was too warped from the concussion-bolts that had battered it to be opened again. Safe, until someone found him or until they decided to finish the job of destroying the stables. . .

He put his weight on the heavy lever, and the hiss of steam that escaped it was drowned out by the frenzied bellow of ten dozen wyverns who had just been given their freedom.

Elani screamed as the bull lifted its head and roared. Inside the pit, the noise was ear-shattering.

Ryushi and Kia fell back, their hands flying to their ears, and scrambled away from the suddenly excited creature.

It had taken a long time for them to calm it down, before its life-long training had mastered its nervous energy. This bull wyvern was a prize stud, a beast which Banto had bought from another breeder because its parents were both top-flight racing wyverns; it had been conditioned since birth to accept riders. Banto refused to have it Bonded – and therefore named – because that sometimes interfered with the beast's ability to breed, and he wanted a clutch of fine racing wyverns from this one. Still, it was usually only Banto that rode it. All this meant that it took a while before the bull decided that the smell of Ryushi and Kia was close enough to a human that it trusted, and lowered itself into a flat squat to allow them to attach the harness to it.

But the sound of the females escaping was too much for it, and it had bellowed in response to their calls. Through the thick walls of the hub, their stampede was too faint to be audible to the humans over the general chaos, but the wyvern's keener senses picked it up. Ryushi had only just secured the last strap when it reared, and they were lucky to get away from its stamping feet and writhing flanks.

"What's up with it?" Elani cried.

"Stay back," Ryushi ordered, snatching her away from its pounding feet.

Pressed against the wall with the others, Elani looked at the raging beast, full of fright and misgiving. "Are you sure we should ride that, Cousin Ryushi?"

"It's safe, El. Me and Kia have ridden before."

"A *bull* wyvern?" she said, eyeing it doubtfully.

Ryushi scraped his hands through his hair and laughed nervously.

Kia, next to them, had fallen coldly silent. She hadn't said a word since she had agreed to help Ryushi get the harness on the wyvern. Now it was there, a complex series of straps and buckles that held three curved, hardened-leather seats in place, one in front of the other, along the raised, bony ridge of the creature's spine.

The sky was suddenly rocked with a terrific explosion, and the walls of the pit shook. They stopped still, even the wyvern; a moment later, there was another one.

"They're bombarding the stables!" Elani cried, clinging to Kia's leg. Kia shook her off impatiently.

"Makes sense," she said. "Why waste their own troops when they can attack from a distance?"

"You think it'll take the weight of all of us?" Ryushi asked Kia urgently. "I've never ridden with more than two before."

"Of course it will," she replied tersely. "They can carry six times us. But we need three more seats."

"Kia, we can't wait any longer!" Ryushi cried.

"Where's *Ty*?" Elani moaned.

"He'll be here any second, now *shut up*!"

"Kia! You calm the wyvern while I open the iris lock!" Ryushi ordered.

"But the others. . ."

"Just *do* it, sis!"

Kia hesitated for a moment, about to argue, then changed her mind and nodded in short agreement. Ryushi ran to the elevator, slapping the trip-lever as he did so. With a bellow of steam, it began to rise slowly, carrying him up to the balcony level. He had barely reached the top before a third bolt ripped into the stables, this one much closer at hand. The bull had gone quiet below, cowed by the renewed onslaught. He could hear Kia whistling on her Bonding-stone, the hum soothing the beast below.

The iris lock control was right next to the elevator. He staggered out on to the balcony, off-balance from the last blast, reached around and pulled it down. Nothing happened for a long few seconds.

Ty, I hope you came through for us, he thought.

Then a great grinding clank of machinery started up above them, and he was jumping back into the massive, wyvern-sized elevator and taking it down to the pit floor.

"Get on!" Elani was howling at Kia, urging her towards the wyvern, who had squatted down to accept riders again, all the time keeping its clear amber eyes on the iris lock on the ceiling.

But Kia wasn't moving. A last-minute attack of reluctance had seized her. "We can still get them!

We can still go back for Father! And Takami! And what about *Ty*?"

Ryushi sprinted from the elevator. "Get on, sis! The second that bull sees a way out, it's gonna go for it, with or without us!"

"But *Father*!"

"*You can't help him now!*" Ryushi yelled over the steadily increasing volume of the iris lock's mechanism and the howls of the rampaging wyverns, some of which had escaped the stables and were sowing havoc outside. Kia stopped arguing as she realized what the sounds meant.

"Ty! He let the females out!" Kia cried.

"Then let's make his sacrifice count," Ryushi muttered to himself.

Kia folded, almost seeming to diminish then, and began to tremble; but Ryushi wouldn't allow her to quit yet. Grabbing her arms, he pulled her roughly towards the wyvern, and boosted her up into the stirrups. She hesitated for a second, then swung herself up and strapped the securing-belts around her thighs and ankles and waist.

A wyvern's back was too broad to sit comfortably astride like a horse, so the harnesses were hardened-leather saddles that supported the chest and torso, with pads and straps for the knees and feet. Riders would lie on their stomachs in a slightly raised position, which both streamlined them and allowed the front rider's hands access to the nerve-points on the wyvern's neck with which the creatures were guided.

Ryushi passed Elani up to Kia, seating her in the middle seat, and Kia began strapping her in. Overhead, a circular section of the roof was gradually sliding open, starting as a tiny hole and becoming wider as the many curved sections of metal retreated from the centre. Ryushi could feel the wyvern's suppressed energy gathering in its muscles as its eyes fixed on the prize above: escape. Hurriedly, he swung himself up in front of Elani, slid into the saddle and tied his straps together, yanking them tight with desperate speed because—

"Stay low, Elani!" he cried, and they all bent forward, their cheeks pressed to each other's backs, hugging low to the creature's spine as its wings suddenly folded out and swung upwards, dwarfing them. Then, with a screech of exultation, the wings came down at the same moment that its powerful legs sprang, and it streaked towards the gap in the ceiling like a bolt. Elani screamed as the massive acceleration made her whole body shudder and blew her hair flat against her skull, and she squeezed her eyes tight shut. . .

7

Of a Screaming Spirit

. . . and when she opened them again, they were skyborne.

The bull wyvern burst out of the top of the stables a second before a trio of concussion-bolts streaked into the open iris lock. There was a heartbeat's silence . . . and then the entire central section blew apart, scattering girders and plates of iron like leaves, sending them spinning lazily through the air to crash into trees or other buildings with deceptively deadly force.

For Elani, Ryushi and Kia, the world was a deafening whirlpool of confusion. The wyvern was racing upwards, howling and spinning as it rose, heedless of the riders on its back. The world blurred and spun sickeningly around them.

Elani was shrieking again, her hands clutched tightly on Ryushi's belt.

"Get it under control!" Kia yelled, her eyes squinting against the rush of wind.

Ryushi barely heard her, but he got the gist of what she was saying. Leaning forward, battling through the resistance, he searched with his hands for the nerve-points on either side of the place in the wyvern's spine where its long neck met the joints of its first, smaller pair of wings. Domestic wyverns usually had the scales rubbed off in those spots, for ease of control. He spidered forward with his fingers.

Should be just . . . here!

The wyvern banked with a screech, coming out of its crazy corkscrew ascent into a long, looping arc, levelling out low to the ground. It took a few moments for them to reorientate themselves, but when they did, they saw that their peril was far from over yet. The sky was thick with wyverns, fleeing from the wrecked stables and winging away from the battle; but three of their airborne attackers had marked their escape amid the chaos, each carrying an Artillerist with a force-cannon mounted on the harness. Their escape from the hub had not gone unnoticed, and the red-armoured Riders were urging their war-wyverns into the pursuit.

"Get us out of here!" Elani squeaked.

"Not yet!" Kia cried, and her voice had a ragged edge of desperation, as she clung tenaciously to the last shreds of hope. "Just one pass! To look for Father!"

Ryushi was having trouble controlling the bull as it was. Bull wyverns were faster and stronger than the females, but took less easily to instruction by unskilled hands. He had the feeling that they were going mainly where the wyvern wanted to go, and he was just there to offer suggestions as to the direction.

Nevertheless, he sent it into a low, flat glide; and the wyvern seemed to agree. They skimmed over the top of the stud, speeding past the smoking husks of buildings they had once known and loved and thought would be there always. The black, insectile forms of the King's Guardsmen prowled the dusty ground below, looking up in surprise as they flew by, close overhead. Some were battling the escaped wyverns that were rampaging around the stud, attacking friend and foe alike; some were guarding groups of workers who had been rounded up and held captive. As they swept towards the western edge of the compound, Kia suddenly shrieked and pointed downward.

"Father!"

He was there, standing proud and defiant, surrounded by Guardsmen with their halberds pointing at him, the hum of their spirit-stones indicating their readiness to strike. And somehow, over the chaos and the noise of the wyvern's flight, he heard her, and looked up. For a moment, their gazes met; and he smiled, his eyes suddenly welling with tears of joy as he saw his children.

And then a soldier stepped forward, wearing close-fitting, ornate armour of dark green. On his face was a mask of silver, fashioned in the effigy of a screaming spirit, its eyes full of anguish and its mouth distended grotesquely. A black ponytail hung from his head to the middle of his back, and in one hand he carried a nodachi – a long, slightly curved sword, its blade limned in bright sunlight. The other soldiers stepped back from Banto, still keeping their weapons trained on him.

Banto turned away from the children, to face the frozen metal countenance of the warrior that stood before him. For a moment, he looked into the eyes of the man behind the mask. Then he closed his eyes, bowing his head in honourable resignation. Without a sound, the nodachi swung into the air, pausing for a moment, quivering on the verge of. . .

Kia went cold with horror as she saw what was about to happen. *"Fatherrrrrr!"* she cried in anguish, and then Ryushi banked sharply away, turning the wyvern northward and blocking the sight below them. They caught a momentary glance of the glittering blade as it began its fatal descent; and then they were away, and there was only the terrible noise as it struck.

"Father," she whispered, tears sheening her eyes.

A moment later, a force-bolt screamed through the air a few feet in front of them, a near-invisible ripple of energy that would have blown them apart had it hit them. Ryushi jumped, looking over his shoulder, and there were the three wyverns that had witnessed their escape in close pursuit. Gritting his teeth, he forced down the tide of emotions that battered at him, and turned his thoughts to retreat.

"Okay," he said, his voice trembling. "Let's see how fast you *really* are."

The bull screeched, its huge wings powering it through the air into a climb. It was a racing wyvern; it was born and bred for speed. Now was the time to use it. Accelerating away from the destruction below it, it soared over the rim of the valley and into the mountains, and in a few moments Osaka Stud – their home and the only place they had ever known – was left behind them for ever.

But the King's wyverns were still after them. The sky was torn by another force-bolt; the shot was wide, but they felt the turbulence that it left in its wake. Kia looked back, her eyes blurred with heartbroken tears, and saw the three wyverns that pursued them, their Riders hunched low to allow the Artillerists to fire over their shoulders. They were falling behind steadily, but not fast enough. Another bolt seared by, too close this time. Sooner or later, the Artillerists would get their range . . . and that would be the end of it.

"Ryushi!" she yelled, over the frightened, huddled form of Elani. "Go lower! We need cover!"

Ryushi glanced back over his shoulder at her, his blond quills whipping around his head, and nodded. "Hold on, El!" he shouted, and then dug his fingers into the wyvern's nerve-points, sending it into a steep dive towards the mountain peaks below.

He could feel Elani's grip tighten on his belt as the rocky ridges and valleys rose up to meet them, terrifyingly fast. He wasn't quite sure what he was doing; only that he trusted more to the wyvern's ability to fly than to his own. It seemed to need little guidance from him, and it appeared to know exactly what he intended. Oh, if he were only Bonded. . .

But all such thoughts fled his head as the wyvern plunged into a canyon between two rearing mountains, and suddenly the rushing air around them dropped in pitch as they raced between the enormous walls that towered above them. Two of the King's wyverns were following closely; the third stayed high up, watching for any move to escape. Ryushi loosened the pressure of his fingers on the wyvern's nerve-points.

"I hope you're up to this," he muttered.

As if in answer, the wyvern screeched and dropped still lower, swooping mere metres above the canyon floor. The rock beneath them melded into a great grey blur. A force-bolt slammed over their heads, hitting rock and blowing up a geyser of powdered stone which momentarily blinded them as they sped through it. The Artillerists' shots were wilder now, as the riders concentrated more on manoeuvring in the tight spaces and less on keeping steady.

"Look!" Elani cried, thumping Ryushi's shoulder and pointing ahead. Rushing towards them was a junction in the canyon, where a narrow cleft split off from the main gully. It was barely narrow enough to admit a wyvern with wings at full stretch; getting through it would be impossible for a novice rider like Ryushi. He began banking the wyvern gently to the left, steering it along the wider route.

Another force-bolt, this one hitting the ground behind them and throwing out another plume of rock powder, obscuring their pursuers' view for a moment.

And suddenly the bull wyvern swooped to the right, banking hard, ignoring Ryushi's instructions. Elani shrieked as they shot towards the narrow defile, and her arms flew instinctively up in front of her face . . . but then they were arrowing through, the canyon on either side looming high above them, scarcely a few feet between the wyvern's wings and the rock walls. The wind resistance was terrible here, and they clung on to each other for dear life, fearing that they would be swept off the back of the creature if they didn't, harness or no harness.

Behind them, there was a screech and a dull *whoomph*. One of the pursuing wyverns had banked too late and winged the edge of the defile, sending it careening into the canyon wall. The force-cannon had been destroyed on impact, exploding everything nearby.

But the second Rider had made it, and Kia watched with disbelief as he spurred his wyvern after them through the cleft. The Artillerist was taking aim again, levelling his own force-cannon for another shot; and this one only had to get *near* them to knock them into the wall and send them plummeting.

Elani seemed to sense the danger, turning against the gale to look behind them.

"Cousin Kia!" she yelled, her voice seeming thin and faraway. "Use your stones!"

Kia's spirit-stones began to charge even before she had comprehended the words, drawing invisible energy from the rock walls, beginning to glow a dark, fiery red. She had little power left within her, after the escape from Osaka Stud, but it would be enough. It would have to be enough.

The Artillerist sighted down his cannon.

Kia felt the tingling, crackling sensation in her body, and reached out with her thoughts, meshing with the slow, ageless rock of the canyon wall, sending herself into it, making it shake, making it *blow*.

On either side of the canyon wall, just in front of the pursuing wyvern, the rock blasted inwards in a cloud of dust and boulders. The wyvern flew right into the hail and the passengers were battered on all sides for the shortest of seconds . . . but that second was all it took. The Rider lost control, the wyvern's wing clipped the side of the defile, and the force-cannon shot went wildly astray. The wyvern crumpled as it hit, spinning downward in a flailing ball of wings, and hit the bottom with the same dead *whoomph* as its companion.

Ryushi hadn't noticed any of this. He was hardly breathing, his eyes fixed ahead, not even daring to try and guide the wyvern in case he should distract it. The knife-stroke of sunlight at the end of the gully was all he was looking at, his heart thumping as it grew wider, wider . . . and then it swallowed them, and they burst out of the canyon, soaring up into the sky and away from the mountains, Ryushi letting loose a great whoop of joy, and—

His exultation was suddenly arrested as he saw the third wyvern, swooping down from the sky to meet them. He had forgotten about that one. The blank red visor of the Rider hunched lower as he spurred his mount on towards them. Ryushi took control again, digging his fingers into the nerve-points which influenced the wyvern's foremost set of wings – the small ones, used for guidance – and banked to the side as the Artillerist let a force-bolt fly.

Ryushi was beginning to understand the Artillerists now. They shared his ability to create concussive force, but they were weaker than he was. They had to focus their power through a force-cannon. That amplified the energy, but also limited it. They could only fire in a straight line.

Ryushi didn't have that problem. And it gave him an idea.

He took a deep breath, reaching inside himself. He had drained his stones when he had saved Elani in the family house, but his strength had largely returned to him by now. If he could muster enough for just one strike, just *one*.

"You *can*," Elani said, her quiet voice in his

ear; and it seemed as if she had known exactly what he was doing.

He was too high up in the sky to draw any energy from the earth. He would have to make do with what he had. Relaxing his grip on the wyvern, letting it fly itself, he began to concentrate.

It started as a warm, solid core inside his body, just below his heart. From there it thickened, grew layer upon layer, until it was spreading burning tendrils through his limbs, filling his skin, crying for release. He channelled it into his hand, holding it within his clenched fist.

The enemy wyvern was in front of them, looping around for another attack.

He threw it out with all his force, a bolt of energy that streaked away from his hand, searing towards the enemy. The Rider saw it at the last moment, banking his wyvern sharply . . . and it sped by just beneath the creature's right wing, leaving them unharmed.

"Cousin Ryushi. . ." Elani said, a strange sort of defeat in her voice.

"Wait," he said. "It's not done yet."

In the distance, the bolt was arcing around,

turning back on itself and heading once again towards the King's wyvern. The Artillerist was lining them up for another shot; the Rider was intent on his dive. Neither of them had seen it.

"Come on, come on. . ." Ryushi muttered quietly.

Faster it came, closer and closer, catching up with the wyvern even as it sliced downwards to meet them.

The Artillerist's thumb hovered above the firing stud.

Impact.

The explosion echoed across the mountains. Ryushi levelled out their wyvern, feeling the terrible exhaustion settle on his shoulders from his drained stones. Together, they watched the last of their pursuers fall, spinning silently towards the peaks below, a trail of smoke following them down . . . before it feathered in the wind and was finally swept away.

He bit his fist to try and stop the hot, shameful tears from coming; but nothing would hold them back. Alone, Ryushi sat on a sun-dappled rock under the canopy of the trees and cried bitterly.

In a stroke, his life had been swept away. His father, his brother, Aunt Susa, his cousins, his friends, his *home* . . . all had gone. He and Kia had been cut away from everything they knew, and thrown out into the world with no direction, no purpose, and no understanding of what awaited them.

He wished it all back, as if wishing hard enough could have made it so. More importantly, he wished his sister were with him . . . but his only source of comfort in this tragedy was not interested in his grief.

They had landed on a forested plateau, where they could lead the wyvern under cover. They needed time to rest and gather themselves, and deal with the feelings that threatened to burst out from within them. But by the time they had landed, the tears that Kia had shed at their father's death were dry. Her eyes were clear, hard and cold. She had no compassion for her brother's sorrow; instead, she stalked off into the forest. Elani had stayed with the wyvern; she was only a few dozen metres away, for Ryushi hadn't wanted to leave her alone. But he didn't want her to see him cry, either. Tears were for boys, not for grown men . . . and though he was neither, he was old enough to feel the shame of his grief.

It seemed like a long time he sat there, thinking the same things over and over, letting his grief and rage seep reluctantly out of him, his tears washing the poison clean. The faces of his family, the times they had together, the hardships and the good times . . . his whole life had been Osaka Stud. And now it was no more.

But one thing stuck in his mind, pricking at him like a pin. The creature in Elani's room. The thing that had claimed to be an emissary of King Macaan. It had called him the son of a traitor. It *could* have been lying, but . . . had their father really committed treason? No, it was impossible. Not Banto; he had always sworn that King Macaan was the best thing that had ever happened to the Dominions. But the King's Guardsmen were a peacekeeping force, dedicated to justice. He couldn't believe they would commit such a terrible act without some kind of reason. And why were they after Elani, an eight-winter *child*?

He hung his head. He didn't understand any of it.

He was deep in his sorrow when he became aware of Elani standing in front of him. He tried to wipe his eyes, but then decided that it was not worth the effort.

"I'm sorry," she said, and there were tears on her own cheeks.

"What have *you* got to be sorry about?" he said, a little cruelly.

Elani's gaze fell to the ground, and she was silent.

"Do you have anywhere to go?" he asked at length. "Anywhere we can take you?"

She looked up at the leaves above. The sun was heading westward now. "There *is* somewhere I have to go," she said.

Ryushi sniffed. Once again, she was talking with a determination and surety that belied her age. "Where?"

"Hochi's place, in Tusami City. He'll look after me. And you, if you want."

"Hochi? Father's business associate?" he asked thickly. "Wasn't that who he went to meet last time he went away? When he came back with you?"

Elani nodded gravely, the motion seeming comical coming from an eight-winter child. Then she looked up at the sky again, as if she could see through the branches of the trees, the flat oval leaves of the kujas and the spiky green-and-red shivers of the ukakis. "They'll be coming before nightfall," she said. "When those Riders don't return, they'll look for us. We had better be gone by then."

Ryushi rubbed the back of his hand across his eyes. He felt tired, tired and heart-weary, but he knew that what Elani said was true, and he could not allow himself to wallow in his grief. Banto would not have wanted that. He had a promise to keep, and he intended to keep it; and that meant getting the girl to safety.

Wordlessly, he slid down from the rock and accompanied Elani back to where the wyvern waited patiently under the fringe of trees. Kia was there also. They looked at each other; Ryushi's eyes were full of pain, but Kia's were glacial, and revealed nothing.

"We have to go to Tusami City," he said.

Kia tilted her head in acknowledgement.

TATTERDEMALION

MACAAN'S
GUARDS

SPIRIT-
MASKED
WARRIOR

8

Royalists and the Ignorant

Ryushi sat up on the back of the wyvern, straightening in amazement. The slow, steady beat of the wyvern's wings and the rush of wind in his hair seemed to fade to nothing. He breathed an oath, unable to take his eyes off the vista beneath him.

"There it is," Elani said.

They had been flying low to avoid being seen, and so they had not been aware that they were reaching the end of the mountains until the peaks suddenly fell away, and the world spread out before them. Even Kia – who had been responding to everything with the same chill indifference up until now – took a sharp breath.

Before them was the ocean, stretching away for ever, a carpet of glittering azure in the westering sun. On the distant horizon, wispy clouds drifted, the only indicator of where the sea ended and the sky began.

Ryushi had never seen anything so massive in his life. He'd been told of the ocean, sure; his father had even promised to take them when they came of age. But he'd never imagined its sheer size. . .

"We've come off course," Elani said behind him, obviously unimpressed by the spectacle. She'd seen the ocean before many times. "We need to follow the coast round to where the mountains meet the veldt."

Mechanically, Ryushi banked the wyvern to comply. He was still mesmerized by the undulating carpet of light, the hot evening sun glinting off a million distant ripples.

They travelled a little longer, gauging time by the heavy *whoosh* of the wyvern's wings and the heaving of its flanks beneath their harnesses. They had been riding for a long while in the odd, forward-slanted saddles, but both Kia and Ryushi were used to the position, and Elani appeared to be suffering no discomfort.

"Slow down, cousin," Elani instructed. "We're coming up to the city now."

Ryushi could barely wait the last few seconds before Tusami City came into view. He'd heard so much about it; he'd waited so long to go there, to leave the confines of Osaka Stud where he had spent his whole life. He was still reeling from seeing the ocean when, suddenly, Tusami City was upon them.

It had been built at the junction where the mountains abruptly ended and tumbled away into a vast, grassy plain that was thinly forested with strange trees shaped like pinecones. Their lower leaves were vast discs that stuck straight out, with the trunk in the centre, and the discs got smaller towards the top. "Pagoda trees," Elani supplied, but Ryushi wasn't really listening. He was fascinated by the traffic that crawled across the veldt, following the dusty trails that wound away to who-knew-where: covered wagons and ox-drawn carts, rickshaws and carriage-trains; a colourful entourage of conveyances of all descriptions, many of which he had never seen before. . .

But more impressive was the city itself. Built at the foot of the mountains, the buildings and streets swarmed up the rocky faces, a profusion of stone and iron, seeming to cling on like limpets. Chaotic constructions jostled for space within the lap of the mountains, or pooled around the base, where they were protected by a high wall of tar-black iron. Pipes hissed with steam, and here and there awesome towers of metal scaffolding reared out of the confusion, with hammers inside that slid up and down ceaselessly.

"What are they?" Ryushi asked Elani, before realizing how absurd it sounded that he should be asking knowledge of an eight-winter child.

"Magma derricks," she replied, as if it was obvious.

Ryushi made a quizzical noise.

"They tap the lava that runs beneath the mountains," she said. "It gets made into steam. That's how the city gets its power."

"Oh."

"You wanna know something else?" she continued, sweeping her small hand over the sight below them. "This is only two-thirds of

128

Tusami City; it runs right back into the mountains."

"In*side* the mountains?"

Elani smiled behind him, delighted to be able to show off. "Right inside the rock. There's all tunnels and everything," she informed him. "Y'know, this is the last outpost before the mountains. Hochi says that it's the northernmost place in the Dominions except for farms and stables and other isolated places like. . ." She trailed off, biting her tongue. She hadn't wanted to remind him of home. She saw Ryushi's shoulders tighten, but he said nothing. Abashed, she fell silent for a time.

The wyvern began to slow, and Tusami City neared.

Elani guided them down. Though she sounded confident, Ryushi didn't think she was quite as sure of herself as she made out. She seemed to know the city well, pointing out landmarks as they descended; but he doubted that she had ever flown over it before, and navigating from the sky was a lot different to navigating on the ground. He was worried about attempting a landing, but his fears eased a little when he realized that the wyvern, too, knew where it was going. It must have been flown to Hochi's stables before, and had surmised by now that they were going there again.

They descended into the steam and bustle of Tusami City. Spires and buildings seemed to rise around them. Another wyvern winged its way above the streets, sparing barely a glance for them. They touched down in the centre of a wide, circular courtyard covered in gravel, landing with a rough thump. All around were the sights and sounds of a busy stable: the growling furnaces of the nearby hatchery, the squawks of the wyverns, the chatter of the tenders. The stablehands and the beasts that they were grooming did not even look up as their mount folded its wings and lowered itself to allow them to dismount. Ryushi felt a pang of sorrow; it was all so familiar, yet forever gone. He held back the tears that threatened, and began unhitching himself from the wyvern.

As they dismounted, they noticed someone

striding over to them from one of the larger buildings. As he got closer, his steps quickened, until they could make out a tall, broad-shouldered man, with arms like tree-trunks and a great belly barely restrained underneath a simple hemp shirt. The top of his head was completely bald, and the remainder of his hair was gathered in a short black ponytail. He had a great, thick moustache that drooped to either side of his mouth.

"Elani?" he said as he neared them, and the tone of his voice suggested that he knew something was wrong.

"Uncle Hochi," she replied gravely.

His glance passed from her to Ryushi and Kia. Then he waved a meaty hand at them. "Come inside, quickly."

They allowed themselves to be led across the courtyard, trailing behind him. Ryushi was frowning at his back, chasing a thought that he couldn't quite pin down, when Kia suddenly said: "He came to the stud a lot when we were younger," and nailed it for him.

"*That's* where I've seen him," he said, then looked at his sister. It was the first time she had volunteered information since . . . since that moment. He thought again of the silver-masked warrior that had killed their father. "You okay?" he said to Kia.

"Stupid question," she replied.

Ryushi subsided. They were both in a state of shock at the moment, and he knew he shouldn't let the impenetrable skin that his sister had thrown up around herself worry him. He had to worry about himself. At the moment, he was operating in a daze, and the grief and pain felt like it was going to burst out of him any second; but he was burying it as fast as it bubbled up, keeping it down until he had time to let it go. There were bigger issues here than their sorrow, and at the moment it was a luxury they could scarcely afford.

Hochi led them into a small, low-ceilinged room with a window that looked out over the stables. A rough wooden table stood in the centre of the room, surrounded by stools. He collared a young boy who was passing outside, and brought him in with them. He was a bright-faced kid of eleven or twelve winters, with a shock of dark green hair.

"Gerdi! Get word out that Elani is back. I want to know if the King's Guardsmen even *stir*. And send to Calica; tell her to expect us."

"'Kay, Hoch," the boy replied cheekily, and was about to go when Hochi observed to the newcomers: "You look starved." He then added as an afterthought to Gerdi: "Get us some food from the kitchens, too."

"Anything else, Greatest Overlord Master of Kings?" he asked, making an exaggerated bow.

"Yes," Hochi said, his face neutral. "Learn some respect."

"I'll try," Gerdi replied in a tone that indicated he would do no such thing, then ran off.

Hochi glanced at them apologetically. "That boy can get into and out of anywhere in the city, but the *baggage* that comes with him. . ." He sighed. "Sometimes I wonder if it's worth it. But where are my manners? Sit down, please. I can tell by your faces that matters are grave."

"Who's he, Uncle Hochi?" Elani asked inquisitively, as she clambered on to a stool. "I don't remember him."

"He's been away until recently, Elani," Hochi

replied, then added with a strange note of resignation: "But I'm sure you'll get to know him very soon. I doubt you'll have a choice."

They sat around the table, the sunlight slanting in through the windows across their faces. Hochi leaned his huge forearms on the table and interlinked his fingers. "Now," he said in his deep bass rumble. "Tell me what has happened. We have a little time while preparations are made, but we will have to move soon. It isn't safe here for you. If your enemies found you once, they'll know this would be the first place you'd head for."

The story was told in haste. Elani took the brunt of the burden, with Ryushi occasionally interjecting. Hochi asked questions, but they had no answers for him. They knew almost nothing beyond that the stud had been attacked and destroyed by a fleet of the King's wyverns and a cohort of his Guardsmen. They did not know what had happened to those who had surrendered. They did not know what had become of Ty (the mention of his name made the muscles around Kia's eyes tighten, but no more).

They did not know why the stud had been attacked. But their father was dead; that they knew. The admission almost made Ryushi cry again, and he struggled doggedly to contain himself.

Hochi looked sympathetically from Ryushi to Kia, his small brown eyes studying them. "I'm going to tell you a story," he said, suddenly appearing to come to a decision. "It's about something called Parakka."

"Uncle Hochi!" Elani cried in astonishment.

"They'll find out sooner or later, Elani," Hochi said, in a calm, reasonable tone. "And they have nowhere else to go. I owe it to Banto."

Elani looked back at Ryushi and Kia, wringing her hands. There was a long silence, before she blurted suddenly: "I'm sorry I never told you! Hochi made me keep it a secret!"

"Told us what?" Ryushi asked, bemused by the conversation.

Right at that moment, there was a knock on the door. Hochi got up to get it. It was a couple of the kitchen-boys, carrying trays of food. They came in and laid them on the table, then bowed and left. Ryushi hadn't thought about his stomach since that morning; but now he realized that he was famished, and the sight of the spread before him made his mouth water. On one tray, some kind of roasted bird sat in a nest of bowls: sweet potatoes, spiced rice, egg noodles, all kinds of salad and vegetable. On the other, a loaf of honey bread and warm butter jostled for position with a pitcher of cream and a bowl of wine-glazed mountain berries.

"Eat, please," Hochi said distractedly, motioning vaguely at the food. Elani and Ryushi fell to it, but Kia had no appetite. She picked at some berries for a time while the others ate in silence, and then spoke up.

"You'd better tell us about Parakka," she said. "I assume that it's got something to do with Father?"

Ryushi stopped eating, and looked from his sister to their host.

Hochi nodded.

"Then we have to know," Kia finished, holding his gaze steadily.

"You're right," Hochi said. He stood up and

walked to the window, looking out to the yard beyond. "I owe Banto more that I can ever tell you. We all do. I know he would have wanted you to know about what he did. After all, he brought your brother here to see less than a week ago." He paused, and looked at his feet. "The very least I can do for him is to help you now, in any way I can."

They waited for him to continue. He seemed to be trying to think of the words to express what he had to say, but he couldn't find them. In the end, the truth was blunt and honest, told without frill or exaggeration.

"Some years ago, there was a period of unrest in Tusami City. You weren't born then; it was before your time. The reason for the unrest was that there was a widespread famine following King Macaan's assumption of the throne, and the King was taking what little there was for his soldiers. People were starving."

He hunkered forward. "The Thanes of each province in the Dominions held a secret meeting in Tusami City, to decide what to do about the King. Somehow, the King found out about it. He launched an attack on their meeting, but the fighting spilled into a riot. Tusami City . . . well, it wasn't a fair fight. The King's men were fed and armed. The city folk were desperate and starving."

"No one ever told us about this," Kia said flatly.

"Yes, they have," Elani said. "That was when Macaan unified the Dominions and got rid of the Thanes. Only you heard it a little different, I bet."

"That's because the truth would tarnish the name of our great and gracious King," Hochi said, with an edge of cynicism in his voice that made Ryushi frown. "He later said he'd sent his troops in to crush the riot, not that they had started it. Nobody dared say otherwise."

"Except you," Ryushi said insolently, stirred faintly to a challenge. To insult the King was to insult the greatest ruler the Dominions had ever known.

"Yes," Hochi smiled wearily. "You'll find that people such as me and Gerdi have a lot to say about the King that you might not expect."

Kia cut in before Ryushi could reply: "Stop sidetracking him, Ryushi." She looked back at the bald man. "What's this got to do with Parakka?"

Hochi ran his hand across his moustache, then resumed the telling. "After the riots, there was a lot of bad feeling about the King. We'd all heard a lot of things about him, rumours about how he had got to the throne and the atrocities committed in his name. Nobody in Tusami City had really believed them until then.

"That was when a man called Banto appeared. He had travelled, and he had seen the things that people spoke of at first hand. He knew what was truth and what was rumour. And he gathered people to him, people like me, who could not turn a blind eye to the injustices of the new King. He gave us structure. He brought us together. And the seeds of Parakka were sown."

"You're saying. . ." Ryushi began dully.

"Your father was killed because he was a rebel against the King," Hochi said. He looked at Ryushi and Kia to gauge their reactions. Kia's face was blank; Ryushi's a picture of horror and mute shock. Sighing, he went on. "Parakka is the name of an organization of what the general public would call terrorists. But that isn't the right word. We're not terrorists. But what we *are*, is dedicated to overthrowing King Macaan and removing his line from the throne. We're dedicated to freeing the Dominions from his oppression before he gets so much of a stranglehold on us that we can never shake him off."

"Father was . . . a *traitor?*" Ryushi said dumbly. The words of the creature that he had saved Elani from in the house came back to him, calling him *the son of a traitor.*

"No!" Hochi shouted, whirling and slamming his huge fist down on the table. "*Traitor* is a word for royalists and the ignorant!"

"And we are both," Kia put in blandly.

Hochi looked at her, her pretty face impassive, and felt the anger drain out of him. He straightened again, looking down at them beneath bushy brows. "Yes, that you are," he said, his voice smaller. "It's my duty to correct that."

"Royalists?" Elani cried. "I mean, you *used* to be, but . . . you don't still support the King after . . . after what he *did?*"

Ryushi shrugged, looking at his sister for support but finding none. He turned back to Elani. "The King is *good;* even Father used to tell us that.

He's done great things for the Dominions. I can't believe he'd ever do anything like . . . the things you say he's done. Not unless it was done without his knowledge, or he had good reason, or—"

"Stop that now, boy," Hochi growled, and his voice had taken on an edge of menace. He seemed to loom over the table. "Your father told you those things because it was safer for you to believe that the King was our benefactor; that's why he told you the 'official' version of Macaan's ambush on the Thanes. You know that to speak out against Macaan is treason. If your father told you the truth, and you went shooting your young mouths off . . . well, a loose word in the wrong ear, and you just might disappear. You'd be far from the first." His brows darkened. "But if I ever hear you *dare* to imply that the King had 'good reason' to kill a man like Banto again, I might just forget my *duty* long enough to thrash you senseless."

The harshness of his words shocked Ryushi into silence, and he looked at his hands, ashamed. At the same moment, the door swung open and Gerdi popped his head in, a cocky grin beneath a mass of green hair. "There's a runner gone ahead to Calica. And you're not gonna like this, boss, but we got wyverns sighted over the north mountains, coming this way. I think they'll be your guys."

"Alright," Hochi said, standing up suddenly. "Clear this place, save what you can and then follow us. And don't get caught!"

"Look who you're talking to," the boy replied. "As if they'd catch *me*."

He disappeared again. "How did they—" Elani began, but Hochi interrupted her.

"From what you have told me, all the signs mean one thing. Banto was betrayed. Somehow, the King knew about him, and where you were, Elani. And you can bet that if they knew about Banto, they'll know that this was his last port of call. And they'll be on their way."

Kia turned to Elani. "Where do *you* fit into all of this?" she asked, an accusing edge to her voice.

"Later," Hochi insisted, as Elani went pale. "Right now, we have to go. Calica is the head of our chapter of Parakka in Tusami City. She runs a number of safehouses. We can hole up there until we work out what to do with you. Follow me."

He led them out of the stables and into the throbbing streets of Tusami City. Ryushi was overwhelmed by the rush of people and traffic that barged past him. Rickshaws clattered by, people from all corners of the Dominions chattered and haggled in a hundred different accents, and there was the smell of sweat and dust and oil and animals. The noise around them was a constant sea.

Hochi and Elani seemed not to notice it as they hurried along the twisting, narrow streets of the city, ignoring the hawkers and market-stalls, noodle-stands and sideshows. Kia appeared not to care.

But, Ryushi, bewildered and reeling, could barely take it all in. He just wanted to rest. He wanted a moment of sanity, a time when he could sort out his feelings . . . and he wanted sleep. He didn't know what he was saying or doing any more; he just needed to disengage his beleaguered mind for a time. He and Kia had been pushed and pulled from pillar to post, but both were too grief-stricken to resist or question what was happening to them. They were in no state for this. But it never seemed to end.

They wound their way through the chaotic architecture of the city, labouring under the hot evening sun. Hochi appeared to know where he was going, though Ryushi couldn't imagine how anyone could find their way in a place like this. After a time, they began to ascend, following the steep roads that crawled up the face of the mountain and doubled back on themselves endlessly like snake coils. Dulled to the hectic profusion of life around him, Ryushi was scarcely aware of much of the journey, placing one foot in front of the other automatically as he allowed himself to be herded towards their destination.

He did not know how much time had passed when the road they were following suddenly twisted sharply and plunged headlong into the rock of the mountain, beneath a high, crude archway. All he felt was the relief that they were out of the sweltering sun and away from the crush; for here, the air was cool and the traffic much thinner. They were in a long tunnel, with rows of smooth metal doors on either side, each one inscribed with a numeral. The bright light of the day was replaced by the orange light of the glowstones that were situated at even intervals along the walls.

"These are the living quarters for those who can't afford the rent outside," Hochi informed them, leading them onward. The rock tunnel split and divided, branched and branched again, as Hochi took them deeper and deeper into the mountain. He seemed to be navigating by the inscriptions carved on the stone pillars that stood at every junction, but Ryushi couldn't decipher them and was too drained to try. Eventually, they halted at a door that was identical to any other, except for the arrangement of the numerals carved into it. Hochi felt inside the keyhole and pulled out a tiny strip of orange silk.

"Calica's been here," he informed them. "The place is safe." He produced a heavy key and slid it into the lock, letting them inside.

The house, if that was what it could be called, was made up of several interlinked chambers, some at odd angles to the others. Narrow tunnels led off from the large central chamber, some angling down and other heading upwards. Almost all of them were filled with junk: Machinist parts, chests, books, and other things too strange to identify. Thick, black metal heating pipes hissed steam, providing warmth and making the air feel damp.

Hochi made a quick check of the place to determine that there was nobody there before closing and locking the door behind them, securing them in the orange-tinged gloom of the safehouse.

"She'll be back when she's made the arrangements," Hochi said. "In the meantime, why don't you all get some sleep?"

He took Kia and Ryushi through a short, downward-sloping tunnel that led to a tiny chamber in which there were two unassuming beds. As if the sight of them was a trigger, Ryushi felt the exhaustion and heartache and pain all rush up at once to claim him, crackling like a hood over his skull and pushing him down into unconsciousness. He fell on to the nearest one, and was asleep before his body hit the blanket.

* * *

"Is he all right?"

"He's been through a lot."

Voices. And softness around him: a bed.

"They need time." Hochi's voice. "We can't expect them to get over something like this in a day."

"Have you told them?" This one was a girl's voice. Not Elani, though. Older.

"About their father? Most of it. You know me; words aren't my strong suit. That's your gift, not mine."

"About Elani?"

"Not yet. I was going to leave that to you."

Ryushi was vaguely aware that they were discussing something important, something to do with him. But his mind refused to focus, and the sweet, cloying bed was dragging him down towards sleep again.

"I'm sorry about what happened to your stables," came the female voice. "I heard the King's Guardsmen didn't leave much of it standing."

"We all make sacrifices," Hochi replied mutely. "It was a good cover; but I was no

147

wyvern-breeder. Banto carried that business for me."

A long pause. Then the girl's voice.

"Do you think they'll join with us? Takami wasn't so keen, when you brought him here."

A sigh. Then Hochi's voice again. "I can't say, Calica. But Takami is gone now. Please don't mention him to them."

"I won't." A pause. "When can we move them to Gar Jenna?"

"Give it a few days, Calica. Please."

"It's not safe here. Our security has been compromised. We should get out of Tusami City for a while."

A sigh again. "Tomorrow, then."

"I'm sorry, Hochi. I know how you feel about them. But we don't have time to be gentle."

If other words were said, Ryushi didn't hear them. He drifted into sweet oblivion, and for a time he forgot all about the pain.

Some time later, he surfaced from sleep again, and this time opened his eyes. The room they were in was dark, lit only by a single glowstone on the rough rock wall. There were no windows. He stared at the blackness that was the ceiling and blinked. His lashes came away dewed, refracting the orange light in a blurry dazzle before his eyes. It was then that he noticed his face and pillow were wet. The cold path of a tear raced from the corner of his eye along the ridge of his cheekbone, then progressed slowly down to his ear. A sob hitched out of his chest, seeming loud in the dark room. And then there was a rustling, and he felt Kia lie next to him and put her arm around him, one hand stroking his quilled hair.

"It's okay, bro," she said. "We'll get through."

The words of sympathy, and the relief that his sister had not entirely frozen him out, were all it took to set him off. He hugged her, and cried bitterly for what seemed like eternity.

But though she held him, and comforted him through the night, Kia's eyes were dry, and no tears gathered there.

9

Some of Them Left

They were awoken by rough hands, shaking them hard.

"Get up!"

It was Hochi. The windowless room was still dark, but the orange light outlined his huge body and bald head. They had fallen asleep fully dressed, having no other clothes; now they muzzily disentangled themselves from the warm embrace of sleep.

"Come on! We have to go now!"

There was something in the urgency in his voice that jarred them both into full awareness again. They clambered hurriedly out of bed.

"What is it?" Ryushi asked.

"Follow me!" he ordered sharply, and then turned and disappeared through the door.

They went out after him, through a stony, roughly-carved archway and into the central chamber. They picked their way through the stores of crates and boxes before Hochi opened the thick steel front door and hustled them out, back into the long, high-ceilinged rock tunnel, studded with glowstones, that curved away into the distance to either side of them.

Elani was waiting there, with Gerdi watching over her like a bodyguard, occasionally glancing nervously up and down the tunnel. Their faces were pools of shadow.

"I told you we shouldn't have put them here, Hoch," he said snappily as the big man emerged.

"What's happened?" Ryushi enquired.

"The King's Guardsmen are on their way here," Gerdi said. "Calica got us word. She's trying to—"

"Hold on," said Hochi, holding up his hand. They fell silent. In the distance, there was an faint grinding, growling noise.

"Crawlers," Gerdi hissed. "Coming from both ways. They're on to us, alright."

"Back into the house!" Hochi snapped, and hustled them all inside again. He made a path through the clutter in the central chamber and pulled aside a tapestry that hung in a darkened corner of the room. Behind it, there was a small tunnel, set halfway up the wall and angling diagonally away. It was much narrower than the others – which were large enough to walk through comfortably – and pitch dark.

"Up here," he barked.

"In *there*?" Elani asked, her voice quavering.

"Come with me," said Gerdi reassuringly, patting her small hand. "You'll be fine."

He grabbed a glowstone from a wall bracket and clambered up, taking the lead. Hochi picked Elani up and put her in next; Kia and Ryushi followed, and Hochi went last, with another glowstone.

The stone of the tunnel was rough and bumpy, and they scraped their knees and backs as they went along; but Gerdi set a demanding pace, and Hochi would not let anyone lag. Ryushi was too swept up in the action to feel claustrophobic; besides, he and his sister had always been at home exploring the narrow caves and gullies of the mountains, so this was old stuff to them.

Orange light from the glowstones shifted on their faces, shadows darting and stabbing between the lines of their features.

"How did they know?" Ryushi whispered, when he could bear the silence no longer. Their only sounds since entering the tunnel had been grunts and scratches.

"Whoever knew about Osaka Stud also knew about this safehouse," Hochi replied.

"It's where we store stuff," Gerdi added from up ahead, without looking round. "Supplies and things. And sometimes . . . unusual items, like Elani here. If they find it, it's gonna set us back something special."

"Gerdi! I'm not an *item*," Elani protested.

"Figure of speech," he replied. "Hey, Hoch. Tunnel ends up ahead."

"Thank Cetra for that. I must have scraped myself raw. They made this tunnel too narrow."

"You wanna lose some of that puppy-fat, boss-man," Gerdi commented from up ahead.

"Fat?" Hochi cried, outraged. "I could crush you like an egg, you little runt."

"You'd have to catch me first," came the reply.

"And with all that extra weight on your belly, I wouldn't rate your chances."

The tunnel came out in what could loosely be termed as an alley. It was covered over with a grille, which, Gerdi explained in a self-important tone meant to impress Elani, had been previously loosened to serve as an escape route. There were similar grilles all over the underground section of Tusami City, used to pump air to the deeper caverns where there was no circulation. Parakka had been enterprising enough to tap into the system of tunnels to provide a back door for their safehouses.

They dropped through the grille-opening one by one. Hochi squeezed through last, while Gerdi stood with his arms crossed, tapping his foot in mock-impatience. Elani giggled at his exaggerated display.

They found themselves just off what must have been a main thoroughfare: a wide tunnel, lined on either side with all kinds of market stalls, selling their wares in the orange light. The smell of steaming crabs and fried vegetables, strong incense and fish filled the air. They were in a

➤ **Part One**

small side-tunnel that ran between two covered stalls, hidden from the road, cocooned in shadows.

Hochi replaced the grille, then made a swipe at Gerdi while he was off-guard, hoping to cuff him round the head. But Gerdi was too fast; he ducked it and scampered away, sticking his tongue out.

"You'll have to do better than *that*," he taunted.

Grumbling oaths, Hochi led them between the covered stalls and on to the thoroughfare. Ryushi glanced from the young, green-haired boy to the huge, bald man and back again. Their relationship was a strange one. Gerdi seemed to take every opportunity he could to antagonize Hochi, but even Ryushi – a virtual stranger to them both – could see the affection they shared for each other. It was just that neither of them seemed to be willing to admit it. And though Gerdi would make fun of the older man mercilessly, there was a deference in his manner that betrayed the respect he held for Hochi, just as Hochi's attempt to clout Gerdi reminded him of the bears he'd seen in the mountains, playfully batting their cubs.

They joined the flow of traffic. Ryushi had no idea what time it was, but here underground it seemed that the commerce was in full swing. Once again, they were surrounded by the constant jabber of people, and a heaving sea of orange-hued faces surged around them. They were jostled by a musk-ox drawing a cart. Hawkers and street-children harassed them. They passed a street-vendor, who was boiling spearfish in vats heated only by the power of his spirit-stones which flowed through his hands as he plunged them into the bubbling water. But Hochi would let nothing slow them down; he carried on pushing his way through, and the others followed in his wake. Kia occasionally glanced back at Elani, but she was being watched over by Gerdi, who seemed to have appointed himself her protector for the time being.

"You think they'll follow?" Ryushi asked Hochi, who was intent on barging his way forward.

"They'll think we're long gone when they arrive. I don't think they'll follow. But they'll try to cut off any exit from the mountain. We may have to fight our way out."

The words were meant for Ryushi, but Kia overheard them; and somewhere inside her, a cold, cold flame ignited. The death of her father had rekindled and redoubled her terrible sense of loss after her mother's disappearance. Since the escape from Osaka Stud, she had been numb, unresponsive, and uncaring about anything outside her own desolation. Her brother's tears last night had done something to stir her out of her self-absorption; but the aching emptiness still resided inside her, a vacuum in which nothing could exist.

But suddenly, something *did* appear there. An emotion which she had only ever been vaguely acquainted with before, and which she had never truly experienced in its raw form. Not till now.

Hate. Hate for the people who had hurt her, who had killed her father and brother and family; who had killed Ty, her sweet, unassuming friend; who had destroyed her life. Parakka, the King, Elani, the creature that Ryushi had fought off in the house, Elani's unreasonable fear of mirrors, the destruction of their home . . . it all added up to something, something cruel and huge, something that they were caught up in and had no idea how to escape. But Hochi knew. And she guessed Elani did, too; that naïve, innocent and yet disconcertingly perceptive child.

Someone was going to give her answers. And soon. But until then, there was only one way to salve her emptiness. And that was revenge.

The stones down her spine were burning with power, drawn from the earth all around her. She thought of Hochi's words and she *prayed* that they would have to fight their way out.

The thoroughfare widened after a time, and the traffic became sparser as it got less and less squashed together. A little while longer, and the tunnel roof suddenly swept upwards and away, and they found themselves in an enormous circular cavern, a junction at which several other tunnels of similar size met with theirs. The centre of the cavern was a vast market, a cluster of tents and canopies of all different colours; while around the outside, a great ring of traffic circled it, bustling into and out of the tunnels. Across the market from where Hochi and the others walked, the cavern was open to the outside air, and the brilliance of the midday sun beamed in, swamping the faint luminescence of the glowstones.

Hochi pulled them aside from the main flow of traffic, and they gathered around him to listen.

"Now look, this is only one of six or seven exits out of the mountain. We have no idea how hard the King's Guardsmen are looking for us, or whether they will have the exits covered. But if there are too many of them, don't try it. Pull back, try not to be seen, and we'll head for one of the other ways out. In this game, we play for opportunity . . . we don't need a confrontation here. You understand?" He addressed this last to Ryushi and Kia.

Ryushi nodded automatically, but there was no real conviction in it. He was still confused. All his life, his father had taught them – no, *everyone* had taught them – that the King was good, and kind, and that his soldiers were there to protect the innocent and uphold justice. It was hard enough to be asked to ditch all that he had learned, even in the light of what had happened to them; harder still was the idea of attacking the

King's Guardsmen. Before, at the stud, it had been self-defence. But now? He didn't know. He didn't know what to believe any more.

Hochi looked at Kia, awaiting a response. She gazed back at him coolly. "I asked if you understood," he repeated.

There was a pause, a few long moments as their eyes locked. Then Kia smiled quirkily. "Of course," she said.

Ryushi watched her, doubt in his eyes. She understood, all right. But she didn't agree.

Hochi was satisfied, though. He didn't know her as well as her twin. "Okay then. Now we didn't have any time for disguises, so we're going to have to rely on Gerdi to get us through. Follow my lead."

Gerdi sighed, cocking an eyebrow. "Where's Calica at, anyway? If she was here, *she'd* have a plan. Meathead here just leaves all the work to me."

"What can *you* do?" Elani asked.

"What can *I* do?" Gerdi replied. Elani blinked, and suddenly she was looking at an exact reflection of herself, which stuck out its tongue in her face. She yelped in shock and jumped back; but then there was only Gerdi, with his odd green hair and impish smile. "Give me a minute, then follow after," he said to Hochi, and then was gone.

"What was *that* all about?" Kia asked, looking from Elani to the departing boy, who was melting into the crowd.

"Didn't you *see*?" Elani said.

"See what?" Ryushi replied.

Hochi snorted. "That's why the boy's so blasted good," he said grudgingly. "He's half-Noman. Born in a Noman village, and given Noman stones at his *pah'nu'kah*." He glanced at Ryushi and Kia. "That's the name for the birth ceremony when you—"

"We know what a *pah'nu'kah* is," Kia said dryly. "We weren't *that* sheltered."

Hochi coughed to cover his embarrassment and then looked back at the younger girl. "Anyway, he can make you see pretty much anything he wants when you look at him."

"He looked like *me*!" Elani wailed, profoundly disturbed.

"So why didn't we see him change?" Ryushi asked, further confused. "Or any of this lot?" He motioned at the milling masses that surrounded them.

"He wasn't showing you," Hochi said. "Just Elani. It's a finite talent, just like anyone else's. He can't make it work with too many people at once. I've seen him do it with three, four maximum."

"What's a Noman?" Kia asked Hochi.

"You don't know?" Hochi exclaimed, surprised. "They live out on the steppes in the East, trading tribes that move around as and when they want to. They don't have much contact with the rest of the Dominions. Anyway, the steppes are a great wide swathe of grassland, a very open country. Not a lot of cover. It's said that the Nomen learned the art of disguise as a way of creeping close enough to herds to catch a few before they ran. Others call it a matter of survival, a defence against predators and so on." He shrugged. "Doesn't make much odds to me. They're a slippery sort, at best. I've heard there's some that can make themselves invisible to the

162

naked eye." He paused, looking out over the crowd again.

"So how do you know Gerdi?" Ryushi asked, vaguely interested now.

Hochi looked awkward for a moment, his eyes restless. "I found him when he was young. I caught him breaking into one of our safehouses. He didn't know about Parakka then; it was just a coincidence. I didn't know where his parents were and he's never said. But . . . well, I knew he wasn't going to last long if he kept going the way he was going. So I took him in. Seemed the decent thing to do." He coughed, and averted his gaze from Ryushi's smile. They tried so *hard* to conceal their affection, these two. "Anyway, I taught him the ways of Parakka and it's brought me nothing but trouble ever since. Now it's time to move. Remember, no confrontation if you can help it."

"What about weapons?" Ryushi asked, grabbing Hochi's arm as he was about to plunge back into the traffic. "Me and Kia lost ours."

"If all goes well, you won't need weapons," Hochi said. "If it doesn't . . . well, Banto told me enough about what you two could do." He paused, looking out over the crowded cavern. "It better not come to that."

They muscled their way back into the flow and joined the swirling ring of people and vehicles that edged around the outside of the central marketplace. Keeping their heads down, they jostled towards the vast cavern mouth and the sunlight.

As they neared, their hearts sank. The King's Guardsmen were on to them, alright. Grouped all across the mouth of the cave were the black-armoured figures, dark eye-lenses glaring out of their blank facemasks, halberds at the ready. Kia's eyes flitted over them appraisingly. She reckoned that the halberds worked in the same way as the Artillerists' force-cannons. The Guardsmen generated concussive power in their spirit-stones, in the same way as Ryushi did. But the average Guardsman's power was much less than that of her brother – she guessed they had only two stones, which was the general standard for a foot-soldier – so they had to focus it through their halberds to make it stronger. There had to be some kind of Machinist device at work there.

Also stationed at the cave entrance were two enormous, cylindrical-tracked vehicles. Takami had mentioned these to her, when he had been dropping hints about his visit. Crawlers. They were a nightmare of dirty iron and oil, with a complex array of drill-bits at their forward end. Originally used to hollow out the caverns that went back into the mountains, they had found a new lease of life in the service of the law.

Her eyes picked out Gerdi, as well. He had made no move as yet; he was obviously deciding how he could tackle the problem.

"Keep walking," Hochi said out of the corner of his mouth, over the bustle of the crowd. "There's no way we're getting out of there."

But Kia didn't hear him. She was ignoring the sound of his voice, the milling of the people around her, the hot breeze from the cavern mouth, the enticing smells from the market. She was intent on those blank black visors, the faceless Guardsmen looking left and right, searching. The same anonymous men who'd killed her father and Ty; who'd destroyed their home.

She didn't get angry. That was Ryushi's style, not hers. She had always been the calm one. And so, very, very calmly, she clenched her right fist together and began to concentrate.

Her mind leaped involuntarily back to the days when they were younger, Elani's age or less. Banto had employed a Master to teach them how to use their spirit-stones. His name was Zu-jin. A tall, thin man with a receding head of grey hair and kindly eyes, he was a forgiving and understanding teacher. She remembered his soft, silken voice, as he conducted their lessons in the grassy clearings on the far side of the valley, their skin warm in the mid-afternoon sun.

"Remember this," he said. "The power is not yours. It is never *yours*. You are just a channel. The spirit-stones make you a bridge. You can vent the power through your body and mind; you can even store it, holding on to it until the time is right. But you cannot *create* the power. That" – he squatted down and patted the turf at their feet – "comes from here."

"From the ground?" a young Ryushi asked, squinting in the sun, his blond hair already out of control.

"In a manner of speaking, yes," Zu-jin replied, straightening. "From the planet, and from the planet's *life*. Everything is fluid, self-repeating, self-renewing. Birth and death; plants and animals; predators and plant-eaters; insects and flowers. The cycle of the planet is a constant process of creation and degradation, only to create again. Everything works in harmony. The way of the world is constant movement, constant change. There is a *Flow*. It runs all around us, beneath the earth; it gathers in rivers of energy, which we call ley lines, where the Flow is the strongest. And tapping that Flow is what allows us to" – he opened his hand, and a tiny flame puffed into existence and hovered in his palm – "use the power."

"Ohhh," Ryushi cooed, not really understanding. Kia hadn't really understood then, either. She had been too young. But as time went on, things had become clearer.

"There are many types of stones," Zu-jin continued. "Each has a distinctive colour, and each can affect the world in a different way. Ryushi: though your power, like everyone's, comes from the earth, the earth is not yours to manipulate. Your power can be raw *force*, can smash a tree or a boulder . . . but it can also be gentle, to turn a key in a lock or sew a picture in a frame."

Ryushi's face lit up at the first instance; he didn't seem so keen on the second.

"Whereas yours," Zu-jin continued, turning to Kia, "is the power to move mountains. The soil is your weapon; the rocks are your fists. You can make a flower grow, or make the very ground rise up against your enemy."

Kia remembered feeling disappointed then. The soil? Rocks? It wasn't a very glamorous power for a girl to possess. But as time went on, she realized that her first estimation of what she had fell short of the reality. Used creatively, her power was far more versatile than that of her brother. And it could be just as dangerous.

"Sis, what are you doing?" Ryushi asked warily from behind her, his voice bringing her back to the present. The stones were hot on her back, humming with energy. Some people in the crowd behind her had noticed, for she was wearing the same midriff-revealing top she'd had on when she'd met Ty yesterday, and her stones were beginning to glow. A general hubbub was gathering, and people were backing off.

Hochi turned around, noticing what was happening, and his face froze in horror. "Kia! No!"

But she was already doing it, sending her mind out into the earth like Zu-jin had taught her, *becoming* the little specks of dirt, gathering them together, moulding them, shaping them to her needs. She felt the shift and ripple of the ground as it churned eagerly under her control. The cold fires of hatred leaped within her, but she kept them ruthlessly reined, serving her needs. She was not angry, oh no. But she *hated*. And those Guardsmen that were blocking their escape were going to pay for what their comrades had done.

A sudden shriek went up on the far side of the cavern mouth, and people began running frantically to safety as the ground suddenly began to cave in beneath their feet. The Guardsmen watched, stunned, as the soil of the newly-cleared area fell into a small crevasse; and from that crevasse, a vast arm of dirt and mud and roots emerged. The cavern erupted into panic as an enormous golem levered itself up, a shambling hulk of rock and soil and debris, bellowing as it stood to its full height, towering over the fleeing men and women.

"Kia, what are you *doing*?" shrieked Elani.

"There's innocent people here, curse you!" Hochi cried, amid the howls of the fleeing people.

"She can't hear you!" Ryushi cried, jumping to her defence. "She's working too hard. Let's just take advantage of the distraction and get *out* of here!"

Hochi's face set. He didn't like it, but there was no other way. Enough people had seen Kia's stones glowing to know that the golem was her doing. If they didn't get out now, they weren't getting out at all.

At the other end of the cavern, the Guardsmen had opened fire on the golem. Their weapons were having pitifully little effect on it. The holes that they blew in its soft body quickly closed up, and it kept on advancing on them, roaring as it stomped closer. The Guardsmen began to panic and break, but too late; the golem tore into them viciously, swinging a massive hand down and smashing one of the armoured figures, crushing him.

Ryushi looked away, feeling ill. His sister's face was blank; but her intentions showed clearly enough in the golem's actions. He heard it as it ploughed into one of the Crawlers, heard the shriek of metal as it began to tear apart the outer shell to get at the soldiers inside, and closed his eyes. Then he put an arm round his sister's waist and began to hurry her towards the other side of the cavern mouth. She ran with him on automatic, her mind elsewhere. Hochi swept Elani up in his arms to protect her from the rushing panic of people buffeting past them, and they began to shoulder their way through the crowd towards freedom.

The cavern floor jutted out into the sunlight in an immense, flat balcony, from which several roads and paths descended into the jumble of similar balconies that had grown on the mountain face. Most of the Guardsmen had by now either joined the fray with the golem, firing uselessly at it from a distance, or fled. The heaving crowd swarming out of the cavern in an attempt to escape the battle provided perfect cover for them. Gerdi appeared, as if from nowhere, at Hochi's side.

"Good plan, boss," he said sarcastically. "Real subtle."

Hochi silenced him with a blazing glare, and they kept on going. They almost crashed into a pair of Guardsmen, who were shoving through the other way; but Gerdi stepped in, shouting at them to get over there and deal with that monstrosity. Ryushi didn't see what the Guardsmen were seeing, but he assumed he had taken on the guise of a high-ranking officer. The soldiers obeyed, barging away in the opposite direction towards where Kia's golem was sowing havoc. There was another sickening crunch as the crazed creature flung a soldier into the rock wall with a force that pulverized him inside his armour.

Kia, what's happened to you? Ryushi thought. *What happened to the sister I used to have?*

And then they were into the sunlight, and the feel of the heat on their skin was glorious.

Shouldered and barged this way and that, they relied on Hochi – with Elani still in his arms – to use his great bulk to open a path to where they wanted to go. He took them down a narrow set of stairs in the rock, across a short balcony, and then down to another one. The shrieks and roars of the carnage behind them faded. After a time, Hochi pulled them aside into a narrow alleyway between two houses.

"Stop her," he said, looking at Ryushi, his brow heavy.

Ryushi turned to his sister. "Kia? Hey, sis. Come on, now. It's over. Stop it. Kia? *Kia?*" He looked worried. "Kia? Stop it, okay? Snap out of it?" He patted her cheek, first gently – which produced no response – and then he slapped her, hard. Her head rocked back, and then her eyes focused again, fixing on him with an expression of terrible anger. She grabbed him by the shoulders and shoved him against the other side of the alley wall, her teeth gritted.

"I had it *under control,*" she said, in a voice low with menace. "There were still some of them left."

173

Ryushi gaped back at her, unable to think of what to say. She had never reacted like this before, not about anything. *Some of them left?*

Hochi broke into their confrontation, his deep tones the voice of reason. "We still have to get out of the city. Save it."

Kia glared at him for a second, then released her brother and took a deep breath. "You're right," she said; but the words came out reluctantly. She looked at Ryushi and smiled humourlessly. "Sorry."

"Kia, what is *wrong* with you?" he breathed.

"I got us out of there, didn't I?" she replied harshly, turning away.

"Yeah, you sure made me look redundant," Gerdi commented, with his usual dose of tact. Hochi tried to cuff him again, but Gerdi seemed to possess a sixth sense where the big man was concerned and had already moved away.

Kia fell silent, her arms folded, a scowl marring her face. Hochi watched her for a second. She knew what he thought: that she'd been wrong to start a battle around so many innocent people. But he just didn't *understand* . . . the raw *hate* she felt. . .

174

"What?" she snapped, realizing they were all looking at her. "Let's *go*, shall we?"

They let Hochi lead them after that, heading down the chaotic architecture of the mountain face into the thickly-twined streets of stone and iron at the base. Occasionally they had to duck off the roads when a patrol of King's Guardsmen prowled by, their black armour making them look like tall, sleek beetles. But while these patrols kept them always tense and on the lookout, in a city this size it was easy to get lost in the crowd. They made their way quietly among the bestirred populace, crossing the city undetected.

"Where are we gonna go, Hoch?" Gerdi asked, after a time, as they rested in a deserted stone-flagged back road.

"The main gate'll be guarded. They won't let anyone out without checking them. We'll have to get out through Ritsu's tunnels."

Gerdi blinked. "We can't do that! Don't you think they'll have it covered? What if *Ritsu* betrayed us?"

Hochi's brow furrowed, and he rubbed the back of his neck as he thought.

"Listen," Gerdi said. "They found Osaka Stud and Elani. They seized your stables not long after we left. They found our safehouse." He stamped his foot. "There's *nowhere* we can go that we can be sure hasn't been compromised. We can't even lie low for a while. I *hate* this."

"Come sundown, this city's going to be shut down tighter than a rat-trap," Hochi said. "We have to get out now. Until we're sure of our members, we can't rely on anyone else for help. No Parakka safehouses or escape routes."

Elani stepped forward. "Then it's up to me," she said.

Hochi laid an arm on her shoulder, dwarfing it under his meaty fingers. "Can you do it? All five of us?"

Elani smiled. "Easy." She looked up at them, holding out her hands. Gerdi and Hochi took one each, and offered theirs to Ryushi and Kia. They followed suit, joining their own hands to form a circle. Elani's wide, dark eyes travelled from Ryushi to Kia and back again. "Sorry," she said under her breath. "I'm sorry for everything."

And then the sun went out.

Where is Elani taking Ryushi and Kia? Is it somewhere safe, or are things about to get a *whole* lot worse?

There's only one way to find out...

Read

Broken Sky

Part Two

Turn the page for a sneak preview. . .

1

Weights and Counterweights

"*You*," said Kia, pointing an accusing finger at Elani, then moving it towards Hochi and Gerdi. "Or you, or you." Her voice was icy calm, but tinted with a quiet menace. "One of you is going to tell us everything, and tell us *now*."

Ryushi looked in amazement at his sister. The others were no less taken aback. He still couldn't get used to the radical change in Kia's personality since the destruction of Osaka Stud. But that aside, he agreed with her sentiments. He was confused, and afraid, and didn't know who to trust; and he couldn't begin to get his feet back under him until he had solid ground to stand on. Before they could even start to get over the tragedies they had witnessed, they needed stability. And they needed answers.

Kia leaned towards Elani, her face a mask of shifting shadows in the light of the firepit that blazed between them. "How about *you*?" she asked. Elani looked like she was on the verge of tears.

"Kia, you're scaring her," Ryushi said.

His sister ignored him. Elani trembled. Everyone else stayed silent.

"Now Elani, I want you to answer me straight," Kia said slowly. "I want to know where this place is that you've brought us. Let's start with that."

Elani swallowed, and looked to Hochi.

"Don't look at him," Kia snapped. "Tell *me*."

"Kia—" Ryushi began, but she held out a hand to shut him up, without taking her gaze from Elani.

"Tweentime," she said in a small voice.

"What?" Kia prompted.

"*Tweentime*," Elani said, louder, her face becoming childishly defiant. "The people who live here are Kirins, and they call it *Kirin Taq*, but *I* call it Tweentime. O*kay*?"

Kia sat back. "Okay," she said more gently. "Now we're getting somewhere."

* * *

Ryushi had not known where he was immediately following the moment that the sky suddenly went dark. One second, they had been on the hot, sweaty streets of Tusami City, where the walls were of grey rock and iron; the next they were standing in the midst of a city of sleek black stone, and the sky overhead was not the azure blue of a hot Dominions summer day, but a velvety purple. The sun was no longer bright, but rather it was in a state of eclipse, with only a blazing corona surrounding the dark disc of its centre. It was cool, the temperature of a summer's night, and torches burned in their brackets along the alley, the kind that used to be used in the Dominions before glowstones were discovered.

Kia and Ryushi were struck dumb by what they had just experienced. Was this what the world outside Osaka Stud was like, the one their father had warned them about? A catalogue of impossible and confusing incidents that made a mockery of everything they had learned during their sheltered upbringing?

The bustling world of Tusami City had disappeared. No longer were the streets crowded with a constant flow of traffic, with people from all corners of the Dominions jockeying for space. Here, the streets were quieter, even peaceful. At each end of the alley, they saw passers-by, strange folk with skin that was a dark grey, like ash, and disconcerting eyes with cream-coloured irises swimming in a sea of white. Their hair, Ryushi observed numbly, tended to be shades of red or blue or silver; but the colour was natural, not dyed as was the fashion in the Dominions. He briefly saw one of them riding on the back of an odd, leathery-skinned, two-legged beast that stood semi-upright, with small, vestigial front limbs held across its chest. He stood there, gawping, unnoticed in the alleyway, until he felt a rough hand on his arm and was tugged back to where the others were pressed into the shadows.

"Don't let them see you!" Hochi hissed in his ear.

"But—"

"*Sssh!*"

Hochi indicated for the rest of them to be quiet, too, and then led them onwards, keeping out of sight. He didn't seem quite sure of his route any more; and eventually Elani gave an impatient tut and, pouting, took the lead. She appeared to know the city far better than Hochi, and headed through the alleys and streets as if she'd walked them all her life. Under her guidance, they had no trouble avoiding the grey-skinned people of the city, especially as the streets were so sparsely travelled.

As they moved through this new and unfamiliar place, Ryushi noted that the architecture was completely different to anything he had ever seen before. Rather than the towering, ugly metal constructions that he was familiar with, he saw curves and arches, smooth lines, all made of a strange black stone that threw back the flickering light of the torches in a shiver of tiny flames. There were no hard edges to the architecture; everything was rounded.

What is *this place?* he thought.